DRAGONFIRE!

CODY'S WAR BOOK ONE

STEPHEN MERTZ

WOLFPACK
PUBLISHING
— EST 2013 —

WOLFPACK PUBLISHING
— EST 2013 —

Paperback Edition
Copyright © 2019 Stephen Mertz

Published in the United States by Wolfpack Publishing, Las Vegas

Wolfpack Publishing
6032 Wheat Penny Avenue
Las Vegas, NV 89122

wolfpackpublishing.com

Cover design by Lohman Hills Creative, LLC

Paperback ISBN 978-1-64119-858-5
eBook ISBN 978-1-64119-857-8

Library of Congress Control Number: 2019951378

DRAGONFIRE!

For Jane Moor

CHAPTER 1

The near future ...

The constant, high-pitched whistling of the EA-18G Growler recon jet in flight enveloped Captain Sharon Davis. The steady drone did not soothe her senses, but rather honed them to a razor's edge.

The weather was calm. A beautiful, cloudless day. From above, the sun sparkled off the cockpit canopy. Below, the South China Sea was smooth as polished glass.

This was a routine flight. Captain Davis and Lieutenant Jared Roberts, her systems officer seated directly behind her, were cruising at 10,000 feet, a hundred miles beyond Chinese territorial waters. Of course, no flight was completely routine, Sharon reminded herself. The Navy would hardly waste its resources in tasking a state-of-the-art aircraft and its two naval flight officers if there wasn't a need.

A sonar pattern had recently indicated the presence of a Chinese nuclear submarine in this sector, but a routine follow-through by high-altitude spy planes and satellites had found nothing. This was considered worth checking out, and so Davis and Roberts were dispatched from the aircraft carrier *USS Carl Vinson* to investigate. The Carl Vinson, presently in the region supposedly on a routine training exercise, was in fact patrolling these often disputed shipping lanes.

The day when shipping lanes were at the mercy of submarines was long past. Submarines served a far different role in today's peacetime world. They were in fact a grim way of preserving the peace. The ballistic missile submarines of today served as the world's most reliable means of nuclear deterrence.

These fearful leviathans of the deep stayed mostly hidden in the oceans. Avoiding detection at all costs; always ready for the moment they might be needed. Such submarines were intended to survive a first strike and retaliate. This was meant to dissuade an enemy from ever using its weapons. It was a deterrent that had proven successful since the dawn of what was once called The Atomic Age. Naturally for tactical reasons the placement and movement of such submarines was tracked closely by adversarial interests. The previous week, a Chinese sub had been sighted in this same area but had quickly submerged and disappeared. If Chinese nuclear submarines were on the move, the US Navy wanted to know about it.

As the reconnaissance flight continued on a north-westerly course, Davis allowed herself to savor the bittersweet experience of handling the plane's controls on this, her final mission. She was thirty-three years old, from Columbus, Ohio. Married and the mother of two. And after twelve years, she was leaving the Navy.

Much as she loved flying and serving her country, Davis loved her family even more. Bottom line: her husband and the girls wanted her home. She had come to understand that while serving her country meant the world to her, she'd never again have these precious years to experience the day-to-day raising of her children and the marital bliss that life with a good man like Shep promised. And there were her parents. They weren't getting any younger, either. Mom and Dad had frowned on her joining the Navy all those years ago when she'd enlisted instead of going to college after high school. Oh, they were proud of her achievements, her rank and her service, but to Mom and Dad, a woman's place, especially a mother's place, was at home raising her children.

Sharon would miss having a military career. She would miss the dedicated men and women she served with. But her family tugging at her heartstrings could no longer be denied.

She knew she was making the right choice.

Sharon blinked away these non-essential thoughts, her eyes flickering to the video image projected onto her Heads Up Display mounted over the instrument panel directly in front of her line of sight. The HUD screen presented the upcoming flight path with all necessary flight information appearing as ever-updating text at a bottom corner of the screen. Identical data appeared on Lieutenant Roberts' display.

It had begun to look like this flight was not going to be a wild goose chase. They'd already gotten positive MAD (magnetic anomaly detection) contact. She and Jared were confident that what they'd found was indeed an SSN, the US Navy classification for a nuclear-powered attack submarine. . .but they'd lost contact after tracking for about twenty minutes.

This time they spotted it together on their respective screens.

Davis said, "Bingo!"

Jared's voice was crisp in her helmet earpiece.

"Looks like one of their *Jin* class jobs."

They were closing in fast on a surfaced sub that was like a sleek shadow cruising across polished glass. The sub's speed: ten knots, according to the data printout on her HUD screen.

The submarine's bow carved furrows of white foam from the sea, its bridge rearing above the sea like a huge, slab-sided fin. Forward toward the bow were twelve hatches. The missile launch tubes. Just behind the bridge position were the masts containing the boat's various sensors. Two men were visible on the bridge.

Sharon said, "Ready for our close-up, Mister De-Mille?"

Jared said, "Rolling."

He would be snagging video, the images being relayed simultaneously to the *Carl Vinson*.

Sharon was starting to bank them in for a closer look when something strange happened. Without initial alarm, she noticed a vague certain discomfort. A few seconds later her forehead was beading with perspiration.

She asked Jared almost absently, "What's with our AC?"

"Air conditioning checks okay," he replied. "Trying to scan, possibly reconfigure a software glitch."

During this brief exchange, Sharon began perspiring freely. Flashing warning lights illuminated the instrumentation panels, indicating a shutdown of the environmental control system. Her stomach muscles tightened.

She told herself to remain calm and steady. The supply of air was more than adequate but it was becoming so heated that its intake made her breathless. She felt as though she was suffocating. Trying to stay calm, she wet her lips, tasting salt. She found herself blinking uncontrollably.

She said, "What the hell's wrong?"

Jared's voice came strange, suddenly panicking.

"Sharon, the starboard wing. . .God! It. . .the wing is bubbling!"

The extreme heat was making her dizzy. Nauseous. It required a Herculean effort to turn her head slightly and look out at the wing, which was only a blur. With desperate savagery, Sharon blinked her sweat-drenched eyes to clear them. She looked again.

The airplane's wing was melting into a glutinous mass!

The unbelievable, incredible sight froze her mind. She gathered her wits, forcing herself to speak.

"Eject! We have to bail!"

An otherworldly silence within her flight helmet. She and Jared had lost radio contact with each other! She tried grasping the ejection release. The muscles of her arm and hand did not respond. Flooding awareness swept her mind into sensory overload. Heat like flame blistered her skin. The plane was rapidly losing altitude. The fuselage was beginning to melt!

She must eject! She had to eject! Home. She had to make it home.

Shep and the girls.

Home. . .

CHAPTER 2

Standing on the bridge with his second in command, Admiral Yang had a perfect view of the remains of the US Navy reconnaissance plane, now nothing more than an unrecognizable blob of smoking steel as it plummeted into the ocean. A bubbling, hissing veil of steam lingered where the water had been disturbed. When the steam evaporated, the sea was again calm.

Yang lowered his binoculars.

He felt a pleasurable surge of pride and anticipation. He hadn't allowed himself to feel this sort of emotion in too long a while, perhaps not since his graduation from the Naval Academy those many years ago. The life of a submariner was one of discipline, sacrifice and duty, much of it spent away from family and friends. The ways of life most people knew who did not spend their life in a contained space, serving with other men isolated far below the ocean's surface. Emotion was a luxury such a man could ill afford. Yang was married with a son and daughter but he never thought of them so as to not miss them. But at this moment, he was nearly overwhelmed with feeling.

This was a glorious moment.

Not wishing to reveal his thoughts to the man who stood beside him, Yang retained his stern demeanor.

"Beautiful, was it not?"

The officer nodded smartly.

"Yes, sir. Quite a sight. Amazing!"

"Notify the general. Inform him that the new system has performed admirably."

"Yes, sir!"

The young sailor's enthusiasm was evident. He lowered himself through the small hatch in the floor of the bridge where a ladder led three stories down into the control room in the ship's hull.

Yang smiled to himself, his satisfaction growing. His crew had been carefully, personally selected. While unaware of the details of what was about to happen, they were very much aware that something grand and dramatic was soon to occur and that, by virtue of being a member of Yang's crew, they would be a part of it.

Alone on the bridge, he took a moment to bask in the sunshine. The breeze atop the seagoing vessel soothed an undercurrent of edgy anticipation. With the panorama of ocean and sky enveloping him alone, it was easy to feel as if he was the only man in a new world.

A flagship of the Chinese South Sea Fleet, Yang's command rarely berthed at the Zhanjiang Naval base except for maintenance and upgrading, and even her builders were unaware of the power of this new weapon he had just employed.

The sub was nuclear propelled. The vessel's nuclear reactors could drive her indefinitely around the world's oceans. She was nearly as large as a cruiser. Along the reach of her forepart lay the neat twin rows of circular hatches. Like vents. But these were not vents to allow water into the ballast tanks; they were remote controlled steel doors to allow missiles out. Missiles the destructive power of which exceeded that of all the fleets sailing in the Second World War; great powerful objects that could burst from the deep sea high into the stratosphere and then, in a swift, dreadful parabola of dissent, plunge their nuclear-tipped noses into any city on earth.

Admiral Yang was fifty years old. Stocky of build, his features were stern, craggy. His uniform was always sharply pressed. Commanding an SSNB had been his life for more than a decade. No one had ever seen him crack a smile. The Navy had been his life since the day he'd left the fishing village where he'd been born and raised, destined for the Naval Academy and a life at sea. His earliest memories were as a baby splashing in the pools of water in front of their home after a heavy rain and, as a little boy, making crude wooden toy boats from scraps of wood, that he would take down to the ocean.

His mother, always working. Cooking. Sewing. Scrubbing. Never resting. Grown old before her time. Father. Accompanying him fishing when Yang was old enough to work the nets with the men of the village. Though born of the peasant class, life had imbued in him early a sense of responsibility, duty; of the importance of applying oneself wholeheartedly to whatever endeavor one has committed to. His intelligence and ambition had distinguished him early on in his modest community. When he reached his late teens, the Chinese Navy had been in a state of rapid expansion. He'd left his village, and was surprised at how circumstance and his determination opened doors for the fisherman's son.

A chuckle passed from Yang's lips as he stood there on the bridge, enjoying the view and what he felt. His parents were deceased and he could only imagine how proud they would be to see the heights to which his discipline and ambition had carried him. They would never know. . .but the world would know!

The world was about to change. The planning, the incredible amount of preparation, was complete. Seventy-two hours from now the world would become a far different place. . .

The pleasure he had taken in bringing down a US recon jet, watching its unrecognizable wreckage disappear without a trace into the sea, was as nothing compared to the building anticipation he felt when he thought about what was coming next. He had always been a man of ambition. He had risen through the ranks to become Admiral in record time. Yet a hungry ambition that had always burned deeply within him wanted more.

Only seventy-two hours...

Admiral Yang made his way down the ladder, into his ship, sealing the hatch after him. He gave the order to submerge.

Within minutes, the undisturbed waters of The China Sea were again calm, mirroring the sunshine.

CHAPTER 3

The moonless night brought rough seas to the Pacific.

The mighty Japanese supertanker *Ocean Song* powered effortlessly through the storm. Sixteen hundred feet in length with a beam of two hundred feet, heavy with two million barrels of oil, she plowed through the roiling, towering waves at twenty-four knots, a behemoth of the open seas, unhindered by the fierce weather.

A US Navy four-man submarine broke the surface from the thrashing black depths, stealthy and practically invisible, speeding undetected alongside the looming tanker like a minnow pacing a great white. The speedy little sub bucked and heaved against the storm's fury, tenaciously pacing the supertanker.

The miniature submersible, equipped with Doppler navigation system and sonar, had been designed for covert penetration of enemy territory using water. The submerged ride had been smooth enough after being deployed from the host sub that tracked them unseen from a distance, but now a lieutenant, his copilot tense at his side, struggled mightily to steer the sub, white knuckles against the thrashing turbulence of the storm that battered the small sub without mercy.

Jack Cody didn't give a damn. Only one thing mattered to Cody. *Accomplish the mission!*

Cody was the only passenger. He was outfitted in water-resistant scuba black with a single oxygen tank breathing apparatus, a diving mask that would give him at least some edge in coping with the ferocious elements. His hands were encased in a pair of adhesive gloves, recently developed by the Navy's high tech branch. Working on an electromagnetic adhesion principal, these powerful gloves had only recently been introduced to field work, having been designed exactly for this sort of mission. His footwear, resembling a slightly oversized pair of brogans, was identical in design and function.

The copilot, a cherub-faced Petty Officer, gave Cody the thumbs up sign.

It was time to do the impossible.

A sailor reached up and rotated the overhead hatch. The interior of the sub caught some of the roiling seawater not diverted by the hatch cowl, accompanied by the near-deafening roar of the storm.

Cody lifted himself through the hatch, into the storm.

The sailor scrambled to rotate the hatch shut. He caught only a fleeting glimpse of Jack Cody before the hatch was securely closed.

An incredible sight!

The man in scuba black, his gloved hands and his boots securely bonded to the towering hull of the supertanker that howled through the night, began his perilous climb, practically invisible against the dark-black, storm-battered hull of the tanker.

The young sailor felt as if he was sending a doomed man to meet his maker. He'd observed the passenger's expression during the ride from the host sub. He'd seen some hard cases in his time but never one with such cold, lifeless eyes as this big guy, as if Jack Cody had already been touched by Death itself and yet the man still somehow continued to keep breathing and living and pushing on.

Funny, thought the sailor. After the time spent in such close quarters, and after being so aware of the guy's dangerous aura, he couldn't even remember the color of the man's eyes, only the danger that had shown in them.

The mini-sub angled away, diving. Disappearing into the dark, choppy waters.

Cody set himself to his grueling hand-over-hand ascent up the curved hull, the equivalent of climbing the face of a building several stories high, made worse by the driving, relentless elements. A frigid spray needled his straining arm and shoulder muscles and the portions of his face not protected by the facemask. With nowhere on the smooth hull for his feet to find purchase, his entire weight and upward movement strained under the excruciating physical effort of his ascent.

According to the intel that had brought him here, traveling aboard the *Ocean Song* was Hadi Abu, one of the world's most wanted Islamic terrorists, en route to Japan to initiate an act of terrorism aimed at discouraging the US military presence in the region. Intelligence indicated the intended but as yet unspecified terrorist act was expected to result in a death count in the thousands.

Cody's mission—that is, if he survived this climb—was to *not* kill the terrorist but to apprehend Hadi and turn him over to US authorities for interrogation.

The blackness of night and the storm completely enveloped Cody on his climb. The adhesion gloves were holding even though the wind kept trying to wrench him bodily from the hull and toss him aside into the beyond. But he held on and continued climbing. At one point he felt certain that he'd reached his limit. He was sure he would tumble into the black vortex swirling around him, never to be heard from again. But he kept on. And at long last, he dropped cat-like onto the ship's deck.

The storm blew nowhere near as vicious up here on deck as it had during his climb. The wind and rain whistled, but the deck itself, thanks to the sheer bulk of the ship, remained as steady and stable as a stretch of solid ground.

He sought partial shelter beneath a row of lifeboats where he paused only long enough to shed the scuba gear.

Jack Cody was a big man, well-proportioned and ruggedly built, with thick black hair that was just beginning to turn gray at the temples. His black attire worn beneath the scuba suit made him almost invisible; one with the night. He wore a 9mm Beretta M9 in shoulder leather and a combat knife sheathed at mid-chest for fast cross draw.

He scanned his surroundings, searching out all that might lurk there. Beyond the superstructure extended the incredible length of the supertanker. No more than forty feet separated him from a companionway that led below deck.

Cody discerned the silhouette of a man standing watch this side of the hatchway. A shotgun was worn by a strap over his shoulder.

Hadi's cover was as a member of the crew, though word was he was enjoying a First Class crossing thanks to the amiability of Mrs. Qian, widow of one of the shipping conglomerate's owners. He would not be expecting trouble from the outside. Those aboard this ship did not all trust each other, hence a shotgun-toting sentry whose position confirmed the target's location. The terrorist had not been seen in public in almost a decade, thanks to cover provided by sympathetic high dollar "friends" like Mrs. Qian and her late husband, who had been linked to the Triads, the Chinese organized crime syndicate. Although the mighty tanker sailed under Japanese registry and ownership, the real money behind the firewall of false fronts came from a Triad based out of Hong Kong.

No more than forty windswept paces separated Cody from the guarded hatchway that, if his intel was spot-on, would lead him to the target. Cody sprinted fast and low toward that hatchway on black shoes designed to make no sound, wet or dry.

He took the sentry out with one swift judo chop to the neck, letting the man's unconscious form collapse soundlessly, but grabbing hold of the pistol-grip Mossberg shotgun before it could clatter to the deck and possibly draw attention.

He had no intention of killing innocent sailors unaffiliated with Triads and terrorists. Intel on the *Ocean Song* crew was uncertain. There were enough shady aspects, though, for there to be little doubt that a small seasoned security force would be operational aboard the tanker. With that taken into account, anyone coming at him with deadly force would be met in kind. But that didn't include this sentry.

He continued through the hatchway, into a companionway carpeted in plush red. The sound of voices, indiscernible, originated from behind a door two down to his left. He strode to that door, advancing quickly. He entered the cabin with a kick that sent the wood panel splintering inward off its hinges.

It was a plush woman's bedroom, warm and close. The storm could only be vaguely heard as if in the far-off distance. There was the smell in here of incense and sex. A king-size bed dominated the dimly-lit cabin, its burgundy sheets rumpled.

The cabin's two occupants reacted in wholly different ways.

Hadi half-sat in bed, his back propped against the headboard by silken pillows. He had a muscular build, and was stripped down to a pair of Speedo shorts. A lazing stud who'd just had his bitch. But his reflexes came lightning fast! He hopped off the bed, filling one hand with a pistol and the other with something snatched off the bedside table, his brutish face twisting into an ugly snarl.

Mrs. Qian was seated at her vanity. A silk kimono hugged her well-toned, shapely figure. Her file claimed she was forty years old but she retained the figure of a girl half that age. She sat with her legs crossed, revealing plenty of golden thigh, brushing her luxurious, shoulder-length hair that was black as a raven's wing. She turned idly to gaze at Cody's entrance with disinterest.

Cody paused with his feet squarely planted, his knees bent to allow him a quick evasive leap though he hoped a shotgun aimed at the guy's middle would discourage resistance. His instructions, after all, were to bring in Hadi Abu alive.

He said, "Party's over, you two. Anyone here speak English?"

He knew from her file that Mrs. Qian spoke English, but Hadi replied before she could. He raised the hand holding whatever he'd snagged from the bedside table.

"Go to hell, American fucker. Do you know what this is?"

"Doesn't matter what it is," said Cody. "Set it down easy, Hadi. The gun, too. You're coming with me."

Mrs. Qian chuckled softly. She never stopped brushing her hair.

"That will not happen," she murmured softly. "Is that not so, my lion?"

Hadi's laugh was a coarse snarl. He gestured with his upraised hand.

"This is a detonation device," he said almost casually. "The whole ship is wired. No one takes Hadi anywhere. A flick of my thumb and this ship blows and we're all dead. Whoever you are, whatever you believe, and whatever they're paying you, it is not enough. *I* give the orders on this ship."

Mrs. Qian purred demurely in a bedroom voice.

"It is so, mighty lion."

"Problem is," said Cody, "I don't care if I die."

Hadi did not flinch.

"And would you die being responsible for the largest oil spill in history?"

Cody briefly considered that.

"Good point," he said.

He shifted his aim a few inches and triggered the shotgun.

The round took off the terrorist's arm at the shoulder. The arm dropped onto the floor next to him amidst geysering blood from the cavity where his shoulder had been. The detonation device, un-triggered, rolled from the hand's lifeless fingers.

A lesser man would have lost control. Gone berserk with such an injury and been relatively easy to subdue. But having his arm amputated with a shotgun only served to piss off Hadi. There was still a chance of extracting him even with the severity of such a wound, but that chance was blown to hell when the terrorist started tracking the pistol in his remaining hand for a clear shot at Cody. Hadi vented pain and outrage in a howling scream of defiance.

Cody sighed, resigned to what had to be done.

Riding the Mossberg's recoil, racking another

round into the chamber, he lifted the shotgun's smoking muzzle another few inches and triggered a round that splintered Hadi's head into shiny red fragments that splattered everywhere. The terrorist's corpse was still collapsing in an ungainly sprawl when Cody chambered another round, swinging the Mossberg on Mrs. Qian.

Rather than appearing distressed at her lover's grisly demise, the woman now stood at her vanity table, having escaped the spray of his blood. She was reaching into a drawer. She froze when she saw the shotgun muzzle aimed at her heart.

"Lady, don't even think about it," said Cody.

She withdrew an empty hand from the drawer and stepped back, eyeing him coldly. Continuing to ignore the burbling mess on the floor.

A ruckus sounded in the hallway outside the cabin. The doorway became filled with sailors coming to their boss lady's rescue. Cody fired the shotgun over their heads. The warning shot had its intended effect. The sailors scurried for cover, leaving the doorway again empty.

Mrs. Qian regarded Cody with a proud, unwavering stare. She was quite a woman. Lovely as a pinup model but with nerves of ice in the presence of violence and sudden death.

"What now?" she asked, as if wondering if they should go to a movie or have dinner first.

Cody considered. It was unfortunate that the mission's initial target had been nullified, but this cold-blooded beauty would likely serve as an acceptable substitute for Hadi. These were international waters; there was an outstanding Federal warrant for her arrest in connection with her company's illegal dealings. She was providing transportation for a terrorist who'd intended to kill thousands of Americans, once they reached Japan. Cody's only option was to work fast.

Keeping her covered with the Mossberg, he withdrew a satellite phone from his pocket and quickly thumbed an autodial, signaling for pickup.

Then he told her, "You're coming with me."

She lifted an eyebrow.

"And if I don't?"

He said, "Close your eyes."

She blinked.

"I beg your pardon?"

Cody did three things in a smooth, fast sequence. He made a loose fist of his left hand and popped the woman a short, fast one to the jaw with enough juice in it that her eyes rolled back in her head. His right arm slung the shotgun by its strap over his left shoulder. His left arm was going to be busy. He wouldn't be able to pump the shotgun. And he deftly caught a KO-ed Mrs. Qian as she did a half-turn and collapsed, out cold.

Cody flung her over his left shoulder. She was so light he barely noticed the weight. With their sudden close body contact, he did notice her warmth and her scent; part sexy perfume but mostly the scent of a woman who has just been made love to.

He thought, *What a waste!*

Cody filled his right hand with the 9mm Beretta from its shoulder holster. With Mrs. Qian braced securely against his shoulder, he hustled out of the cabin.

CHAPTER 4

Withdrawing from the cabin with a woman over his shoulder and a pistol in his hand, his intention was to head straight for the nearest hatchway and the storm-lashed deck beyond, and extraction. . .*if things went according to plan!* Curious Japanese sailors were crouched in the hatchway, eyes filled with curiosity and anticipation. They scattered when they saw Cody and his gun.

He made for the hatchway.

A shot sounded from behind him, magnified by the confines of the enclosed space but not loud enough to drown out the dangerous whistle of a bullet that missed Cody by inches.

His response was instinctual and coordinated. He pivoted, facing the danger. Another report thundered. Another near miss. This round sizzled close overhead, piercing air where he and Mrs. Qian had been seconds earlier. Never losing his firm grip on her unconscious form, he dropped to one knee.

At the end of the short corridor, four tough-looking hardcases bearing hardware had poured in through a hatchway. This would be the professional security force.

Cody's Beretta barked twice.

The pair of gunmen in the lead, who had opened fire on him, each caught a round in the heart area. Dead on their feet, in falling they blocked the way of the pair bringing up the rear. Confusion ensued at that end of the corridor. Another shot sounded from there, sending another bullet.

Cody was already barreling through his hatchway, onto the deck.

If anything, the storm's intensity had only increased while he'd been below. The supertanker appeared to be staying on a steady course, its sheer size and speed cutting through the tempest. Silver sheets of forceful, wind-driven rain blew across the deck, obscuring visibility.

A new sound could be heard cutting through the maelstrom. Indistinct at first, then growing almost as loud as the constant howl of the wind.

A U.S. Navy helicopter appeared, hovering directly overhead. The side hatch door was flung open. A rope ladder, long enough to reach the deck, unfurled from the helicopter to where Cody stood with the unconscious human cargo draped over his shoulder.

He regretted having to holster the Beretta but there was no choice. The rope ladder danced wildly about him in the chaotic blowing crosscurrents of wind and rain. He failed at repeated attempts to grasp and steady the jitterbugging rope. With the pistol holstered, he finally managed to wrap his free arm around one of the lower rungs of the rope ladder.

The instant he'd securely affixed himself to the ladder, it began hoisting him and the woman upward. So far this was a perfectly executed extraction performed by the numbers. But right now was the most dangerous minute or so of the entire operation. He was exposed and vulnerable during this crucial window of time when the rope was shortening, being winched up into the hovering bird. Without his gun, without being able to return fire, Cody was now essentially helpless, suspended on this rope ladder halfway between the chopper and the deck.

An easy target.

He was not the only one to realize this.

Three men toting weapons appeared from the hatchway through which Cody had exited the superstructure. The remainder of the security force hardguys, including the sentry Cody had taken out earlier. The sentry, having regained consciousness, had found a rifle.

Cody could only watch helplessly with one arm

hugging the woman to him and the other hanging onto the ascending ladder. The storm was buffeting him about. His arms felt as if they were being slowly ripped from his body. There was no way gunmen below could miss, not even given the tumultuous conditions.

Cody thought, *So this is how it ends. Thank God. I'm coming, Susan. I'm on my way, honey. I'm almost there...*

That chain of thought was interrupted by explosions that were so loud, they could have come from inside his head. The explosions were in reality, fire from the helicopter's swivel mounted M60 machinegun.

The burst of auto fire mowed down the hardcases. The rifleman was lifted off his feet with enough kill power to toss the sentry over the side, hurling his body into the black void of the stormy ocean.

The other two on the deck were not moving. They'd been literally torn apart by the heavy machinegun fire.

Everyone else on the ship was keeping their head down.

The Navy chopper held its position, oblivious to the storm. The rising rope ladder became even more tumultuous as the backwash from the helo's rotor blades pummeled the air, painfully stabbing Cody's eardrums.

Mrs. Qian chose that moment to begin regaining consciousness.

Cody couldn't hear a damn thing except for the helicopter and the wild, wicked wind that was blowing hard, drenching them in rain. He could feel her body starting to stir slowly against his. He made no effort to speak. He tightened his grip around her, making certain that she was securely held in place over his shoulder.

Then they were aboard.

There was a life-and-death scramble for several seconds, Cody maintaining his balance on the unsteady rope ladder while arms reached out from within the open hatch to draw the woman aboard. Then it was his turn. He was heaved unceremoniously onto the helo's deck.

The hatch slammed shut. The storm again shut out. The helicopter tilted dramatically, the pilot banking away in speedy withdrawal.

Cody gave in to his exhaustion and allowed himself to sink onto his butt somewhat off to himself amidst all the activity, where he could catch his breath.

Mrs. Qian was being attended to by a female flight officer, taking her vital signs and checking for injuries with the economy of movement and concentration of an emergency room nurse. She'd placed a blanket around Mrs. Qian, who looked somewhat worse for the wear. Nothing luxurious about her hair now. It was a water-logged mess, which pretty well described Mrs. Q's condition in general. She appeared not to have sustained any physical injury. There was nothing regal about her now, though she was far from broken. She sat in stony silence, enduring her indignity.

Cody was glad his part was done. He'd brought her in but it would take more than a courtroom to intimidate this one. Even in her current condition, she radiated an inner strength. She would be a tough nut to crack.

A massive terrorist act had been averted with the death of Hadi. For Cody, his breath returning to normal was reward enough. Until the last moment he had harbored a concern that someone onboard the Ocean Song would fire a heat-seeking missile, from a shoulder-held rocket launcher, after their withdrawing chopper. But there had been no more racket from the helo's M60 so it was likely the ship's security force had been wiped out, leaving nothing down there on the supertanker but legitimate crew men and millions of barrels of oil.

For Cody, there remained only one unfulfilled objective.

He was still alive...

Once the chopper was out of harm's way, gaining altitude and moving through the storm with little difficulty, the pilot turned over the controls to his co-pilot. He wanted a look at what all the excitement was about.

He made his way back for a curious glance at the

bedraggled woman wrapped in the blanket. Someone had handed Mrs. Qian a towel. She was drying her hair. The pilot's eyes shifted to the big man in black, off to himself. The big guy didn't seem to notice that he was dripping water from head to foot. The pilot indicated the woman in the blanket.

He said, "She doesn't look much like one male Arab terrorist."

Cody replied without looking at the man.

He said, "Shit happens."

The pilot waited for something else but Cody said no more. The pilot returned to the cockpit.

So that was Jack Cody. He'd heard of the guy.

Hell, Cody had been famous in the ranks even before the tragedy that had changed him. Tours of military duty in the Middle East and every other hotspot you could name. Former Navy SEAL. Jack Cody had become a legend in his own time, rising through the ranks with such distinction as to become point man in the field in the President's war against terrorism.

Then. . .*it* happened.

A tragedy so terrible it would have destroyed most men. But not Jack Cody. He wasn't most men. That was the Cody rep and after witnessing him in action, the pilot was a believer. One close-up gander at the guy and, yeah, the pilot could believe every damn thing he'd ever heard about him. The good and the bad.

They'd come up with a nickname for him, those

who had seen him in action. A nickname no one ever spoke to his face but it was based in a truth and it was why the pilot was especially relieved to be bringing his crew home safe after being part of a Cody mission.

Never, ever to his face but behind his back, those who served on deep cover ops like this with the guy, had taken to calling him *Suicide Cody*.

CHAPTER 5

The Canton waterfront never sleeps. Even at 3 a.m. the wide, sluggish, grimy Pearl River teemed with commercial and private ship traffic of every description from tankers and cargo ships to yachts and private junks like the one in which Phil Hagan waited.

Hagan tried to ignore a slowly building case of nerves that nibbled at his gut.

The contact was late.

In the China of today, a detail like that could mean nothing. . .or it could mean the end of everything. That was the nature of Hagan's world.

A sleazebag named Chua owned the sampan in which they waited. The sampan, a craft of ancient design, is distinguished by its functional, unique shape and the arrangement of its twin sails. Junks of every age ply every waterway of China and always have. Mr. Chua and his modest craft were both in shabby condition, of indeterminate age. Man and boat had seen better days. To the untrained eye he and his boat were indistinguishable from countless others traveling the Pearl, which connected Canton and Hong Kong.

They lurked in the shadows of a dark pier in the heart of the waterfront district.

Hagan knew little about Mr. Chua other than that the man lived by his wits on the periphery of the Chinese underworld, and he could be trusted if the price was right. Hagan had used the seedy-looking hustler and his sampan as recently as a week ago. Chua had family in Canton and family in Hong Kong, or so he said, which is how he explained his travels to the authorities if questioned.

He absently patted his pocket for the wallet he knew was there. The wallet contained a Canadian passport identifying him as an employee of a company in China that was secretly owned and operated by the Central Intelligence Agency. The wallet also held a fake work permit. The money he'd brought with him tonight had already been handed over in payment to Chua.

Hagan had been at this sort of thing for a long time. Too long, he sometimes thought. He'd operated in dangerous, shadowy corners of the world. Danger zones from Kabul to Beijing, from the Latin countries to the Middle East. Hagan knew more than a dozen ways to kill a person without a weapon, and an equal number of ways to persuade an unwilling person to talk. He could lose himself in most crowds, even in a place like China where he was a *qwai*, a "foreign devil"; a "round eyes", in large part because he was a master at adapting to all the ordinary habits of any country he happened to visit.

That didn't mean he had to like these far-off locales to which his work took him. China was so-so but he hated Canton, a smog-smothered urban sprawl of endless apartment complexes and office buildings towering over narrow, busy streets. Canton was a center of Chinese industry. Factories along the Pearl produced automobiles and machinery. Chemicals and food were processed in the city, which stank of industry and greed. There was nothing to appreciate or love about Canton. Its ancient traditional name was Guangzhou, which he found impossible to pronounce. To Hagan, as to most Westerners, it would always be Canton.

He reminded himself that he wasn't here tonight to hate or love this shithole city. He was here to do a job.

Chua's taut whisper broke the gloomy silence.

"They come."

Hagan heard the approaching, rhythmic *chug-chug* of the patrol boat and realized he was holding his breath. He instinctually crouched lower in the sampan, as did Chua, although they were well-concealed in the shadows. Still, this was China. . .

The patrol boat passed, cruising at a moderate speed, its occupants silhouetted against lights from the opposite shore. A man in the bow stood behind a searchlight that panned the river traffic at this late, or early, hour. A manned .50-caliber machine gun was mounted in the stern next to a 400mm gun on a swivel mount.

The patrol boat's chugging receded into the distance.

Hagan resumed breathing.

He said, "Damn. I don't like this."

Chua's chuckle was like pebbles rattling in a tin can. His were the crafty eyes of an old man who had seen much.

"You should be used to it by now, Mister Hagan. For me, it is a way of life, this river. And you know, there is not that much to worry about, eh?"

"You mean your Triad friends? I was told they've greased the machine. You do have good friends, Chua, I'll say that for you. "

The old boatman's nod bespoke an abiding wisdom of the ways of man, reflected in the sag and lines of his weather-beaten face.

"And yet it is wise not to tempt fate."

"A guy like me," Hagan snickered, "I'm tempting fate every morning when I put my feet on the floor, and while I'm asleep too. I just don't like working with amateurs."

"Your friends may have met with mishap. I stay on the river. My element. I am safe. The city?" He shrugged. "They're the police. Bad enough. Too stupid and easily bought-off for even government police work. But the PSB—"

"The Public Security Bureau? That's the provincial law, right?"

"Along the river," said Chua, "the PSB detachment in Canton is known as the most brutal in all of the Republic. Kidnapping, murder, terrible torture. . . There is one man, Major Zhao, the provincial PBS commander." Chua gestured at his own features. He said, "Zhao is said to be the son of the devil. There is a large birthmark across his face like the disfigurement from a flame. It is said that even his superiors fear him. Pray that your friends have not fallen into his hands."

"They're not my friends," said Hagan. "They're not professionals. I don't like it."

He scanned the poorly lighted street at the far end of the pier.

The street, fronted by rows of dark warehouses and cloaked in shadow, ran along the docks past the foot of this pier. There was no one in sight. No movement or sound of any kind except for the river traffic.

Where the hell were they?

The Triad he'd referred to was the 10K Triad, one of the centuries-old Chinese crime organizations based out of Hong Kong. The Triads were a sinister, dangerous presence at every level of the Asian world, much like the organized Crime Family operations in the States. Chua was indirectly somehow linked under the Triad umbrella by being the brother of a cousin of someone in the 10K organization.

China had been riddled with the Triads for two hundred years. The far-flung secret criminal society persisted, but had degenerated far from its roots. Originally a revolutionary society formed with the aim of overthrowing the Manchus and restoring the Ming dynasty, today's Triad societies, like the 10K, which was one of the largest and most violent, dealt in large scale drug trafficking around the world, most of it heroin from China or southeast Asia. They were also involved in illegal gambling, loansharking, arms trafficking, human trafficking, counterfeiting and murder.

The boatman, Chua, had made a specialty of smuggling people out of China for a hefty fee which, in this case was being paid by the US government.

A week earlier, Hagan had connected Chua and his sampan with his local asset at this same pier. The asset was a college kid who was active in a local cell of the national pro-democracy dissident underground.

Political dissent, civil unrest and civil war in a nation with the landmass, population and history of China was nothing new. In recent history, the photograph of a single man resisting authority in shirt-sleeves, with briefcase in hand, standing in the path of the military tank during a political demonstration, was emblazoned forever in the collective memory of the world. That photograph indicated the intensity of an unrest and dissidence that never went away.

After the Tiananmen Square uprising of 1989, the pro-democracy movement was forced underground. Meanwhile the gradual, inexorable, ongoing acceptance of Western ways and values began seeping into China, often in the form of popular culture and fashion. This only accelerated with the Olympic Games in Beijing 2008 and has proven unstoppable in the years since, regardless of trade wars and conservative rhetoric from the Politburo. Ideas like equality, freedom and democracy took on a greater momentum and influence with the young generation as China opened wider to the outside world.

With every incremental step the government took forward, the people demanded even more and it was often because of the influence and rallying of the underground dissidents for social change that they were regarded by the government as a serious threat to law and order. The government employed harsh, often extreme measures in tracking down and suppressing them.

The cell of university dissidents Hagan was dealing with was honored to be dealing with him, a representative of the CIA. Throughout the history of

China, it had always been the Cantonese who were the rebels, the true patriots; exactly what Hagan had been hoping for when he'd taken on this mission.

The human "package" his dissident asset was supposed to deliver to this pier at this time so that Chua could smuggle him out, was a VIP of the first rank; in truth far more important than the person he'd made these arrangements for the previous week.

This was the big one.

The one that mattered.

His name was Dr. Kwan Lieu. He was China's leading nuclear physicist.

And he was defecting to America.

Dr. Kwan had been in hiding. The Internal Security Bureau was searching for him big time, high and low. That's how important Dr. Kwan was. The dissident Hagan had been dealing with, a medical student named Lo, had managed to successfully keep Dr. Kwan hidden, under wraps in a commune near the campus.

The previous week, Chua's passenger had been the physicist's wife. Now it was Dr. Kwan's turn. Having received evidence that his wife was safe in Hong Kong, the physicist was at this moment supposed to be boarding Chua's sampan for the next leg of his journey to freedom, a trip down the Pearl River to Hong Kong.

So where the hell are they?

As if in response to that thought, automobile headlights swept into the narrow dockside street, cutting across its darkness like twin light-sabers, approaching the pier from between the rows of warehouses.

Well all right, thought Hagan.

He rose to his feet in the sampan, again growing tense rather than feeling a sense of relief. This was where everything could go real wrong if it wanted to. Sooner or later a man's luck was bound to run out.

But not tonight, Hagan told himself. *Not tonight.*

Chua asked in a nervous whisper, "Is it them?"

Hagan narrowed his eyes and tried to determine the make of vehicle. Privately owned cars in China were still a rarity except for the upper classes. The average citizen got around on public transportation and bicycle. Automobiles generally bore official insignias or were taxicabs.

At last the headlights drew to a stop at the far end of the pier. In the dim streetlight, he discerned a taxicab of near-ancient vintage.

Feeling a spike of concern that headlights could draw unwanted attention, Hagan muttered under his breath, "Douse your lights, you fool."

Chua tensed up beside him. Hagan knew exactly how the shabby little hustler felt.

Shadowy figures were alighting from the taxi.

Hagan wished he had a gun.

CHAPTER 6

In the taxicab at the dark end of the pier, Mei Chan and Dr. Kwan remained seated. Mei's boyfriend, Lo, stepped from the taxi. The first thing Lo did was to instruct the driver to leave his cab and stand beyond earshot as a security measure. The driver obliged.

Lo said to Mei and Dr. Kwan, "I will ensure that Mister Hagan and the boatman are waiting for us. We must be extremely cautious."

He could be mistaken for someone with a feverish, thought Mei. The sweat on his face shown in the faint lights of the riverfront. She watched Lo walk away, along the pier. Lo had grown tense and irritable during the past few days as this moment drew closer.

She was beginning to reassess her feelings for this young man who'd attracted her attention and affections when she'd first joined the commune. She'd become romantically drawn to this handsome young fellow and his commitment to the pro-democratic underground. After they'd begun trading kisses under the stars, she'd come to learn the identity of the elderly man her new friends were sheltering. Lo was Dr. Kwan's "handler", and he was about to hand over the doctor over to an American CIA agent for transport out of the country.

She became aware that Dr. Kwan was regarding her.

He said, "My dear, I wish to thank you for the kindness and hospitality you've shown this old man during my stay with you and your friends. You especially, Mei, extended real compassion at a time when my heart felt most alone."

"When your wife was sent on ahead of you last week?"

"Indeed. Yuki's love and affection is the fire by which I warm my soul in this cold world. Her lineage is Japanese. Mine is Chinese. And yet such differences become meaningless when love is present."

Mei blinked away a tear. The nation's leading nuclear physicist and he spoke as a poet. Something within her resisted to any cause the way Lo and his friends had. She was too young, she told herself. There was too much in life yet to be learned before putting oneself on the line to the degree they did. Still, she had grown most fond of Dr. Kwan. They'd never once discussed politics or his defection. They shared an interest in

Chinese history. They discussed philosophy in their occasional moments alone in the other's company.

At the moment, Dr. Kwan hardly looked like a wise, erudite, brilliant man of science and letters. His conical straw hat and shabby attire were that of an elderly peasant river man.

Along the pier, a figure had materialized from the direction of a sampan that could be seen. The man intercepted Lo and they conversed briefly. They started walking toward the taxicab together.

Mei's pulse was racing. She'd only agreed to accompany Lo here tonight because she was fond of Dr. Kwan and wanted to say goodbye at the last minute. Yes, she found the aura of secrecy and danger of what was happening here to be rather exciting, which somewhat surprised her. Mei Chan had a good upbringing and a good reputation, she reminded herself. A nice, decent young lady of good breeding sent by her mother and father to the university so that she might become all she could be as a person. . .and here she was, prowling around the dock with dissidents and secret agents!

It was rather exciting!

She said, "Here they come, Doctor, to assure us all is well," and she started to precede Dr. Kwan, stepping from the taxi.

Dr. Kwan gestured with a raised hand.

"Mei, please."

She frowned, caught off guard.

"Yes, Doctor?"

"Do not reveal your presence here."

"But what do you mean?"

"You must trust me, child. This now becomes a very dangerous situation and I will not repay your kindness by exposing you to it."

"But—"

"Mei, there is no time. Do as I say. Now. There, over where the shadows are deepest. Leave from your side of the cab. Wait until your boyfriend has concluded his business and I am gone, and then the two of you can leave together. Please, Mei. For me."

He spoke while gazing deeply into her eyes, with an urgency of command that brooked no response save obedience.

Lo and the man from the sampan had almost reached the taxi. She felt conflicted. She had come here with Lo. Should she not ask him first before doing what the Doctor sat there asking—*no, ordering*—her to do? She must trust this wise elder's judgment, she decided. Lo would understand.

Mei darted from the taxicab without another word between them. Closing the car door after her without sound, she hurried in the opposite direction of where the driver stood smoking a cigarette. She gained the shadows where a nearby dock crane loomed. Mei crouched there, unseen yet close enough to overhear their voices.

Lo was saying, "Doctor Kwan, this is Mister Hagan."

Dr. Kwan had stepped from his side of the taxi to greet them. Though they were blocked from Mei's line of vision by the taxicab, in her mind she could well imagine them shaking hands in a perfunctory fashion.

"Doctor."

"Sir."

Dr. Kwan's voice, pronouncing that single word, was steady, confident yet gentle, serene as ever. Mei would so miss him.

The men began walking toward the pier.

Lo said, "But Doctor, where is Mei?"

Hagan said, "Who's Mei?"

This American's query was terse, sharp; not pleasant.

Mei wondered what would happen next. A tingle of anticipation passed through her and made her smile, watching safely from the shadows. What would her instructors at the university say, what would her mother and father say, if they could see her now? She was *glad* she'd decided to accompany Lo tonight. This was fun.

Suddenly, blinding light flooded the street and pier from high voltage searchlights!

The three men on the pier jerked up their arms to shield their eyes from the glare of the row of searchlights. A line of rifle-bearing soldiers, wearing the khaki uniform of the Internal Security Bureau, stormed into sight, aiming their weapons at Lo, Dr. Kwan and the man, Hagan.

Mei's heart was now beating in her chest like a drum, and her blood ran cold. *What was this? What was happening?* With the scene before her, beyond the taxicab, bathed in the harsh bright light, she could see everything that happened as if it were a play being performed before her on a stage.

Automatic weapons fire crackled from the dark mist at the far end of the pier where she'd noted the sampan, though now the harsh glare of searchlights at this end of the pier rendered their surroundings nearly impenetrable to the eye.

The cab driver tried to run away but the soldiers heard him. Two of the soldiers quickly overtook him. The driver protested frantically as he was physically led to join the line of men regaining their vision under the lights. The gravity of the moment overwhelmed and silenced the driver.

The tableau held like that for several seconds.

Dr. Kwan made a calmly stated request, his voice not loud enough to carry to Mei's ears. He received no reply from the soldiers other than threatening gestures with their rifles to remain silent.

Then from behind the lights, a man strode into view. A slender man of less than average height wearing crisply pressed fatigues, a swagger stick tucked under his right arm. He advanced with the strutting arrogance of command. His most striking feature was a glaring facial birthmark; a vivid, discolored slash of pigmentation that covered almost half his face from the right temple to his left jaw.

A gasp of fear caught in Mei's throat. She had never seen this man before but she knew who he was. Everyone in the dissident underground knew of Major Zhao, regional commander of the provincial PSB detachment. The unspeakable tortures he'd inflicted upon those poor souls unfortunate enough to fall into his hands for interrogation or punishment were well known even to new members of the commune.

Mei wanted to run away but she could not. That would be wrong. She couldn't leave Lo and the doctor. She didn't know what to do. She remained transfixed by the scene unfolding before her. It was like watching a movie with the sound turned down too low.

Zhao stood ramrod straight as a statue. He snapped a command.

Dr. Kwan stepped away from the other men, leaving Hagan, Lo and the taxi driver standing in a loose line behind him. A pair of soldiers each took firm hold of one of the elderly man's arms and led Dr. Kwan away to somewhere beyond Mei's line of vision.

Zhao issued another command.

The soldiers opened fire on their three prisoners. The loud stuttering of rifle auto fire and the strobe-like angry orange lightning of muzzle flashes filled the night. The three men shimmied in unholy jigs of death, their bodies literally blasted apart in showers of gore before withering into a grotesque tangle of bodies in a spreading pool of blood that was a bright, unnatural red under the lights.

With the gunfire still reverberating and the gunsmoke swirling through the air, Zhao strode with a brisk, official stride to the tangle of bodies. He un-holstered his sidearm.

Mei heard a weak plea of protest rise faintly from the fallen bodies.

She wondered who it could be. Was Lo lying there in mortal agony, begging the man for mercy? She knew only that she must flee, yet she remained transfixed in these first moments after the horror she'd witnessed, thought beyond her now. There was the need to escape. . .*so why had terror frozen her like this?*

Zhao leaned down. There were three sharp pistol reports as he delivered a headshot to each of the fallen.

And that's what spurred Mei into action. *They'd find her if she didn't flee now! If they found her, she would be dead like Lo and the others.*

She whirled from that horrible scene, blindly driven by no other impulse but survival. With her second step into the darkness, she collided with a stack of empty oil drums that toppled, clattering loudly in her ears as the gunfire that had swept the pier, drawing the attention of Major Zhao and every one of his soldiers.

They saw her.

Frozen in the illumination of their searchlights, she hesitated for but a heartbeat, long enough to throw a quick glance over her shoulder. She saw the commander shouting orders, pointing emphatically in her direction. She couldn't hear his words but his men were raising their rifles to draw a bead on her! She ran toward the nearest warehouse without further hesitation, rounding its corner just as rifle fire peppered the night air along with the nasty spitting sall pretty good pretty good ound of bullets whizzing close, missing her by inches.

Then the warehouse wall was blocking her from their sight.

She heard Zhao shouting at his troops.

"Seize her!"

She must escape! She must get away from the docks. She didn't know her way around this rough part of town but she would find a way. She would lose herself in these night-shrouded rows of warehouses.

The panic drove her to run faster. Faster than even in the athletic track competitions at the university. Faster than she'd ever run in her life. Her own labored breathing seemed to pound her eardrums as did the rushing of Zhao's men closing in from the darkness in her wake, their bootfalls pounding the pavement.

If she fell into their hands, she would surely die a terrible death!

Mei Chan ran still faster into the Canton night.

CHAPTER 7

It was a beautiful afternoon in Washington, DC. Cherry blossoms in bloom. Temperature in the upper 60s. Sunshine warmed the White House grounds.

From behind the bulletproof glass of the Oval Office, President Martin Harwood regarded the sunny world outside with a stormy disposition.

The chief executive was a vigorous man. At 65 years of age, he looked at least a decade younger. At 5-foot-10, he weighed in at a solidly built 180. His face was naturally round but with strong features and striking eyes that were penetrating and direct. The salt and pepper hair was worn military-style, unfashionably short. The fact that he was an ex-military officer, not a professional establishment politician, had contributed largely to Harwood's being selected as his party's vice presidential candidate. He exuded a straightforward style and grace that the public and the media had taken to.

Three months after being sworn in, he had become president when his predecessor succumbed to a debilitating stroke. Upon assuming the post of chief executive, Harwood had made prompt and drastic changes among his predecessor's staff and cabinet, appointing a close circle of advisors who were not yes people or inside the Beltway pros, but seasoned movers and shakers in their own right. He had a well-earned reputation for toughness and fairness, for principled leadership and bi-partisanship.

This did not mean that everything went smoothly all the time. There were far too many conflicting forces at work in an ever-shrinking world and a nation of 250 million for that to ever be the case.

Harwood was currently hanging fire at about an even 50% approval rating in the polls. The economy continued to take two steps back for every one forward, and America's involvement in the mid-East had only deepened and expanded. There was still no light at the end of that tunnel. The Cold War was over, but its chilled dryness had made the world into a tinderbox, ready to ignite anywhere, at any time.

And now. . .*this.*

"Dammit, I don't like coincidences," the president said to the two men in the office with him. "The Chinese conducting nuke sub operations in the South China Sea, and denying it. That weird, as yet unexplained disappearance of a recon plane in the same area. *And* a defecting Chinese nuclear scientist who's suddenly gone missing. Gentlemen, no way are those three not connected."

Harwood's Chief of Staff, Jim Corbett, had a thinning sandy-haired comb-over. He was bespectacled with a studious air about him.

He said, "Beijing has emphatically disavowed any knowledge of the fate of that recon plane, nor do they acknowledge anything regarding their nuclear submarine operations."

The president returned to the leather swivel chair behind his desk. Corbett and Whit Jones, his CIA chief, occupied armchairs facing the desk.

"We must proceed carefully and delicately," the president reminded them. "After some bumpy spots in the road our relations with China are presently at their best in more than sixty years. They need to stay that way."

Harwood tried not to reveal to his subordinates the indecision that had been troubling him since he'd received word of the recon plane and its pilots gone missing. This confluence of crises was occurring at a most delicate time when relations with China could go in any number of directions, all of them critical to American interests.

The new China had replaced the USSR as a world nuclear power, and the US was willing to do just about anything to accommodate them for any number of reasons such as China serving as a watchdog over North Korea; a moderating influence on that rogue nation, sharing relevant Intel with the US. At the same time, the philosophical divide between the American and Chinese systems was becoming as great as the gap between American democracy and Soviet communism had ever been.

There was constant Chinese computer hacking of American warships' maintenance records, Pentagon personnel records, and so forth. Trade talks? China's idea of doing business was stealing intellectual property, acquiring sensitive technology through business buyouts, fusing their public and private sectors to give their companies an unfair advantage internationally, and currency manipulation. Such fundamentals would never change.

The strategy of Harwood's administration had been to play hard on trade while always keeping the public rhetoric cool and reasoned. But the more the two countries quarreled over trade, and the closer Chinese and American warships got to each other in the South China Sea, over time the less control either side would actually have over events.

"That missing recon plane," said Whit Jones, "has the Pentagon scratching its collective head." The CIA director was a stocky black man in his fifties. "They're not sure which way to move on this and they're waiting on us for direction. The Navy has a dive team in the area and we should be getting results in today on anything they turn up."

"Until then," Corbett added, "everything's being kept under wraps and out of the media with a Top Secret classification. That plane could have gone down due to human error or mechanical malfunction. It happens. Worst case scenario? Chinese pilots could have forced the plane over the mainland and made them land under threat of being blown out of the sky. They could have jammed the radio communication. That's dangerously close to an act of war."

"Or it could all be some spy game ploy by the Chinese," said the president, "their objective being God knows what. Damn. They really are inscrutable, aren't they?" He asked Jones, "What about these coup rumbles your assets in China have picked up on? Could that have to do with what we're dealing with here?"

"I'd bet on it," said Jones with an affirmative nod. "Getting usable intel out of China has always been like squeezing water from a rock. We're dealing with an ancient, adamant secrecy about their internal affairs and problems. But yeah, unsubstantiated indications have been picked up that a coup is likely being plotted. There's said to be an elite cabal of high-ranking military hardliners who are dead set against the rulers in the Politburo. The hardliners feel the rulers are selling out their country to the West."

None of this was news to President Harwood except for how it impacted the crisis at hand. Beijing for some time had been on the verge of virtually doing away with its barriers to overseas investors and capitalism. The military plotters of such a coup clearly recognized that such political and trade concessions, and human rights reforms made in the wake of the collapse of communism in other parts of the world, threatened their long-held power.

The president quietly drummed his fingers on the desktop, the only indication that his frustration was building to irritation.

"Add it to everything else," said Harwood, "and that's why this missing physicist, Doctor Kwan, is so damn worrisome. He even gave us the code word to nail our interest. Dragonfire, and his assurance it concerns a fusion breakthrough that's been applied to a new weapons system. He's offered to provide us with full details once he and his wife receive asylum in the United States. And now he's missing."

"The wife made it out," said Jones. "Doctor Kwan's intended escape route was the same. Local dissidents got him to Canton where one of our people lined up the 10K Triad's pipeline to bring him out via the Pearl River. We've also lost contact with Hagan, by the way; our man in Canton."

"If this coup we're talking about does succeed," said

Corbett, "if a technological breakthrough like this Dragonfire falls into the hands of belligerent military hardliners, which may have already happened, the balance of world peace will destabilize drastically."

From the chair next to him, Jones nodded agreement.

"We'd find ourselves in another arms race; one that we could conceivably lose."

The president said, "Then it's imperative that Doctor Kwan be located and extracted from the People's Republic. That is, if the poor man is still alive. He's got a brother who's a ranking general in the Army, which has made the whole thing dicey from the beginning. I've read the field reports about rumors of a Chinese breakthrough in nuclear fusion. The refinement of a thermal heat pulse system they've been trying to develop using nuclear energy. As I understand it, Doctor Kwan claims not only to have made the breakthrough but also that the technology has already been implemented."

Jones nodded.

"That was his pitch when he made contact," the CIA boss affirmed. "There's no reason to disbelieve him, especially given the effort the Chinese have put into tracking him down. The technology of that breakthrough is stored between his ears. When we get him, we'll get it."

"And then we can neutralize the threat," said President Harwood. "A weapon like that in the hands of our sworn enemies, those hardline militarists? Gentlemen, that cannot be allowed to stand."

"The problem, of course," said Jim Corbett in his overly studious manner, "is that nothing we're discussing has yet to be determined to be fact."

"That's why I'm reluctant to take provocative action like sending in a SEAL team to locate and extract Doctor Kwan," said the president. "China is one hell of a haystack to find that one needle, and the odds against a dark ops operation launched into a highly militarized country like China? Not good."

Corbett said, "Sir, a thermal heat pulse like the one we're talking utilizes energy released from forcing atoms to merge. Something like that is going to result in an incredible array of never before seen high-tech armament. You're right, sir. If unchecked, something like that would place China at least a decade ahead of the US in weapons technology."

"Mister President," said Jones, "I don't much like coincidences either. When there's this much smoke, there's damn sure a fire."

"I see only one option," said Harwood. "I want Jack Cody on this."

The chief of staff and the CIA director winced in unison.

After an uncomfortable pause, Corbett cleared his throat.

"Uh, Mister President—" he began.

Harwood lifted his hand in a placating gesture.

"I know, I know. Wild card. Maverick. Cowboy."

Jones added, "Death-wish."

"I'm well aware of what happened to Cody. . .after what happened to his wife and kids," said the president. "Privately but using classified government resources, he hunted down and executed every one of the terrorists responsible for their deaths. Every step was so professional and methodical, it didn't come out until after it was over because then he fell apart. Placed on administrative leave. And restored to active service only after extensive counseling, time off and after passing a battery of tests to prove that he was fully recovered, healed and ready to return to work."

"True, sir, all of it," said Corbett, "and it's true that Cody was our best man before the tragedy that set him back."

"He's still the best we have," said Harwood. "Enlisted after high school and became an Army Ranger. Served all over the Middle East. Tours of duty in Iraq and Afghanistan. He was The President's Man for my three predecessors who sat behind this desk. He's as well-known in this office as he's unknown to the general public."

Jones said, "With all due respect, sir, Cody's record is not the issue. I agree with you. A damn good man. . .when he was in his prime. But he's wrapped up too tight since coming back, if you ask me, like a time bomb waiting to explode. What if he loses it in the middle of this mission, with everything that's at stake?"

"What if he doesn't?" said the president. "I don't think he will, Whit. I think Cody's not only the best; I think he's the only man for this job, given the circumstances and the restraints we're under on this. So he's presently operational?"

Whit Jones' flat, "Yes, sir," conveyed no enthusiasm.

"Where is he now?"

"He's stateside," Corbett offered. "Just returned from a mission."

The CIA director added, "He was ordered to apprehend a terrorist and bring him in for interrogation. It, uh, didn't work out quite that way. But I'll concede that Cody is one hell of a kick ass operative. Send him to hell, he'll take on the Devil."

"Sara Durell," said the president, "is she still his control officer?"

"She is."

"Good. There's no one better suited to handle him. Get her in the intel loop on this immediately."

"Will do," said Jones, still without enthusiasm.

Chief of Staff Corbett again cleared his throat.

"Uh, sir, you are aware of the stipulation Cody made before he rejoined."

"You mean that he would only accept being assigned to suicide missions, where there was estimated to be little or no chance of survival? Thing is, fellas, Cody has been succeeding on every one of these so-called suicide missions we've sent him."

"That can't go on forever," said Corbett. "It's like suicide by cop. How can we say the man's back to well-adjusted when he's using the missions we hand him, when he's using us to try and kill himself because he's too miserable to live? Sir, he's trying to commit suicide and we're enabling him to do so."

The CIA director groused under his breath, "Beyond that, the guy's a damn prima donna and I don't like having a man like that in the field. I mean, I feel sorry for the man and everything he's been through, of course, but stipulations and the like? I've been against that from the start."

"You're both right in what you say," said the president, "but I don't see where that changes the crisis we're dealing with. China with a new weapons technology? Bundle that in with a coup and a missing physicist who knows the answers and can bring us up to speed. Whit. Jim. This is nothing we can dodge. Our response options are limited. Direct action is required, utilizing the best we have. That is Jack Cody and we all know it."

Corbett's sigh of concession was lengthy.

"Sir, I've got to say when you're right you're right."

Jones grumbled, "I'll sign on long as it's clearly understood that I think Suicide Cody is not a well man.

On this mission, we are sending him to his death."

"Duly noted," said the president briskly without inflection. "Gentlemen, we're done here. I have a scheduled meeting with the Pakistani delegation in," he glanced at his wristwatch, "six minutes. So, to conclude: the mission objective is to find out what happened to our plane and those two Navy pilots, and to get Doctor Kwan out of China. Tell Durell that this is absolute top priority. I want results, gentlemen. With Cody on this, we'll get action and answers. Let's get started."

His chief of staff and CIA director briskly departed the Oval Office, leaving President Martin Harwood alone to indulge in a moment of contemplation before getting on with his busy day. His stormy disposition had lifted, and he knew why.

Cody was on the job.

The time of waiting and worrying was over.

Now the action would come hard and fast.

.

CHAPTER 8

When he walked through the main entrance of *Chez Leonardo*, the most exclusive Italian eatery in DC, Cody drew a glance from every woman in the place.

Sara Durell witnessed it with her own eyes.

They'd scheduled for mid-afternoon, that lag time in even the best of restaurants between the lunch and the dinner rush when perhaps only half the tables are occupied and a more intimate ambience pervades the expensive atmosphere.

There were a few couples enjoying a stolen afternoon date while mostly the clientele at this time of the day, Sara noted, were pairs and small groups of women enjoying a respite from life's stress with good food and good conversation.

At age thirty-four, Sara was, in plain English, a former spy and covert ops field agent who had risen through the CIA ranks to a top administrative position. She'd managed to survive dangerous missions in hostile environments around the world because from the start she'd cultivated remaining constantly aware of her surroundings. And it was not a skill that diminished simply because she was no longer on those shadowy front lines of espionage.

This afternoon in *Chez Leonardo* was no exception, which is why she didn't miss the fact that every woman in the place cast a glance in Cody's direction when he strode in. Some of those glances were fleeting and idle, others lingered, some with mere appreciation and others with what could only be referred to as bedroom eyes.

Cody was a good-looking specimen of manhood and worth a glance, thought Sara and not for the first time. But as with anyone, the man's true measure as a person was found beneath the surface of the form nature had given him.

She'd known Cody since before their professional association. Before she had accepted the assignment to be his immediate superior, his control officer. She knew Jack Cody, for damn sure. This was no ordinary man. For one thing, while he was more of a 100% "man's man" than any guy she knew, he had never once balked at having to take orders from a woman.

When he reached the table and took a seat across from her, Sara could see what she had not wanted to see in his eyes. Something those women she'd noticed giving him the glance would have missed with their quick looks as he passed. They saw the in-shape, well-dressed outer man, sharp but casual, striding with that composed, centered aura of confidence that would interest any woman, and those qualities were real enough. But up close you could look into Cody's eyes, the windows to his soul, and you could see the infinite sadness, the pain of a soul beaten down and resigned to an empty existence of loss and despair. A dark spirit that would have scared away the light-hearted intentions of any who knew trouble when they saw it, appealing perhaps only to any empaths among them.

She flashed him a genuine smile from the heart.

"Hi, Jack. It's good to see you again."

"Sara."

She'd been his wife's best friend; Jack's deceased wife. The sort of weird coincidence that only happens in real life. Carol had worked at a mid- level administrative position at CIA Headquarters in Langley, Virginia which was how their three paths had first crossed. Cody and Carol had gone on to fall in love, get married and have three kids. Sara was godmother to their children.

Back in those days, Sara realized, she and Jack would likely have embraced with a brief hug and cheek touch in greeting. Not this time. Cody's eyes were no longer those of a man who hugged and kissed.

"How have you been, Jack? Did you read the file I sent?"

"Every word."

"How have you been, Jack?"

"Busy. You read the file I sent?"

She had asked a direct question and he'd responded in kind, making it perfectly clear, that he was not here to fill her in on how busy he'd been. They had traded e-files—his mission aboard the *Ocean Song* for her file that briefed him on the Dr. Kwan situation—via the secure satellite link. He was here to receive his mission orders.

That's the way he wants it, Sara reminded herself with a twinge of sadness. He was civil. It was nothing personal. And that's what saddened her. She blinked away the feeling. Jack wasn't disavowing their friendship, but the old Jack was dead. That's what his manner and those eyes were saying to her. And he was right. She was his control officer. This was their only face time before he caught the next flight out. Emotions did not matter.

"Yes, I read your file," she said. "You're being sent to Hong Kong."

Nothing changed in his eyes.

"Makes sense. That's where Kwan was headed."

"All we know for sure right now," said Sara, "is that he's missing. So is Hagan."

A waiter approached their table to take their orders. They each ordered a Caesar salad. Soft drink for Cody, simply water for Sara. They waited until the server had withdrawn beyond earshot.

"I don't know about Kwan," he said, "but you can write off Hagan as dead unless of course he went underground and took Kwan off the grid with him."

"It didn't happen that way," said Sara. "Hagan carried a sat phone and there are other means of secure contact. There could have been a double-cross of some sort from the people he was working with. He would've gotten that through to us. I'm afraid you're right about Mister Hagan."

"What about the dissident underground that was harboring Kwan. Do we trust them?"

"They approached Hagan. They were his assets and I'm not sure he trusted them completely. He went dark before he could pass a contact point for them. We've got dissident contacts in other areas of China but not Canton."

"How do we account for that?" asked Cody.

"Simple enough. The military there is notoriously repressive thanks to an efficient, that is to say extremely brutal, commander; a Major Zhao."

"So if and when I get to Canton," said Cody, "I seek out Doctor Kwan and go up against this Major Zhao on my own. Sounds like a suicide mission. You're on. But you're sending me to Hong Kong. That means you figure the way I figure. This deal could have gone sideways for another reason."

The waiter returned to serve them. Again they waited until they were alone.

"No one at Langley was crazy about using that Triad pipeline," said Sara. "But with the offer from Kwan coming out of nowhere and with Major Zhao in Canton, Hagan had to work fast so he improvised. The pipeline itself has been in place and operational for decades."

Cody said, "My alternate scenario is your Triad pulling a double-cross. They could be the ones holding Doctor Kwan. Maybe he's already in Hong Kong. That's the 10K Triad. One of the worst of the lot. Have they made contact?"

Sara pecked at her salad with little interest. She spoke between bites.

"Not yet, but ransom might not be the motive."

Cody nodded.

"Dragonfire could be worth a fortune on the black market."

"Could and would. Force Kwan to divulge and once the Triad has Dragonfire, let the bidding begin. Allowing Dragonfire to fall into the hands of our enemies is bad enough but consider also that every Third World despot with illusions of grandeur will also want to possess this weapon of the future."

Cody said, "Let's talk about Missus Qian."

"Ah yes, your friend from the *Ocean Song*. They

wanted a terrorist and you brought home a water-logged widow."

"Widow of a ranking Triad member," Cody amended. "How's she doing?"

Sara set down her fork. She'd lost interest in eating.

"Not so well. She was booked into a cell under suspicion based on her alliance with that terrorist. They found her this morning in the shower of her cell block."

"Dead?"

"Dead as they come. It appears she hung herself from the shower fixture."

"I would've thought steps had been taken to prevent something like that."

"Steps were but Mrs. Q was determined, or so it seems. She'd been allowed to make herself present-able after you airlifted her off that tanker. She was back to looking every inch the well-dressed million-airess when they put her in that cell. She was the only one in that cell block, by the way, as an added security precaution. They traded a prisoner jumpsuit for what she was wearing but they let her keep her nylons."

"Bad call."

"She was raising a ruckus. It was late. They didn't want to make it too rough on her. They'd already done enough to alienate her. They wanted her coop-erative for the Q&A."

"Do you think she committed suicide?"

A frown creased Sarah's brow.

"All possibilities are under consideration. If she was murdered, it was done without leaving a trace and made to look convincingly like a suicide. I guess that does make an international organization like the Triad a likely possibility. Her husband was part of that."

"Well, there you are."

"But why would the Triad want that woman dead? Triad membership is strictly male, right? She wasn't a member. She wasn't on the inside."

"Okay, you tell me," said Cody. "Why would a millionairess commit suicide? She was in good health. She had money. Prestige. A hot love life with her terrorist boy toy. She hit a bump in the road when I showed up but with her money she knew that sooner or later some high-priced legal team would get her out from under."

"Okay, let's stay on that thread. The Triad somehow engineered Missus Qian's murder and made it look like suicide while she was being held in government custody. That is what you're saying."

"*How* they did it is for someone else to figure, if they can." Cody's voice was subdued but sure. "As for *why*: her late husband's associates didn't much cotton to Missus Qian playing fast and loose with Arab terrorists. The Triad gangs are out to exploit civilization, not destroy it. The kind of hijinks she was up to draws attention and that's bad for business, don't you know? But mainly they didn't want trouble because of the Kwan deal so to be on the safe side, they snuffed her. Simple as that. Who knows what she might've overheard just by her proximity to those people?"

Sara said, "It's a convincing theory."

"What they don't realize," Cody went on, "is that the very act of silencing her tells us there's something she knew which in turn confirms that there is something to know. Their overreaction tells us there is something to find out and it has to do with Doctor Kwan because right now he's the big game in play as far as the Triad is concerned."

"You've convinced me," said Sara. "We're on the same page. Since we have no leads on Doctor Kwan, at the moment, in Hong Kong focus on the Triad pipeline. Missus Kwan will be worth a visit. A list of assets and contacts has gone to your email account, flight info and reservations included. The Triad boss man in Hong Kong is Yu Cheng."

All right. Cody finished his salad and soft drink.

"What I'm wondering is how this ties in with a missing recon plane and a pending coup?"

Sara nudged her plate aside. Most of her salad untouched.

"Langley is wondering about that too. There are too many sides to this and that makes it quicksand for you. Watch your back, okay?" Then, impulsively, she reached across the table and rested a hand atop one of his. "Good luck, Jack. Please be careful. We'll have dinner here at *Chez Leonardo* when this is over and you're home again."

"You want to come back here? You didn't finish your salad."

"So we'll go someplace else, your choice."

His touch was ice cold. He withdrew his hand. Cody rose from the table. Withdrawing his wallet, he absently dropped enough cash on the table to cover their bill and a decent tip.

"Haven't you heard?" He gave her a humorless chuckle that was more of a snicker. "We make our own luck."

And with that, he was gone.

It was troubling that he had been so cold during their encounter but she accepted it because she'd read his psych report. And she'd known Jack in better times when, between missions, the guy had been a happy and proud family man. Beyond that, Jack certainly knew how close Sara and Carol had always been. They'd often referred to themselves as soul sisters.

As a friend, Sara knew she had Cody's respect because he certainly would have perused her file when Carol first introduced them. Though they never discussed it, Cody would know how she had earned her present level within the CIA through sweat and dangerous missions. Sara had an uncle, now deceased, who'd been an active field agent for many years and who helped Sara get her foot in the door after college. Beyond that, the list of her assignments within the agency and the field ops that had gotten her to her present administrative position were beyond reproach.

Sara had been the last person Carol Cody spoke to before she died. An innocuous, kind of silly phone conversation between two friends. Brief because Carol said she was on her way out the door, taking the kids to school. She'd gotten behind the wheel of the family car, turned the key in the ignition.

The fiery explosion that followed killed Carol and the children in one shattering eruption of unthinkable violence and loss. The high explosive had been wired to the starter.

She watched him walk away—again getting those subtle sideways glances from every woman in the place!—and she could not remember ever feeling more sad than she did right now. Jack and Carol had become her best friends. She'd lost one of them. She did not want to lose them both. She must accept Jack's ways of grieving his loss.

Cody was a damn good man. Decent. Noble. Having trouble? A problem? Call Cody. He could kick the world's ass. And yet all this good, decent, noble guy wanted was to die, to be put out of his misery.

It was hell to watch and not be able to do anything about. . .*except to facilitate.* She wasn't kidding herself. That's exactly what she'd just done, handing Cody his latest assignment. Was she *enabling* "Suicide Cody" in his quest to put himself out of his misery by dying for his country on one last mission?

As his control officer, she knew if anyone could find the needle called Dr. Kwan in a dangerous haystack called China, it was Jack Cody. That was a good bet. He'd been able to set up his strange—some said ghoulish—arrangement with the government because of his incredibly high success rate.

He'd make it home this time, she told herself.

That's when a thought came, unbidden, that surprised her. Could she be falling in love with Cody?

No!

Sara promptly told herself to stop thinking like that.

CHAPTER 9

It was another beautiful day on the South China Sea. The placid surface was a rich turquoise color beneath a cloudless sky.

One hundred miles beyond Chinese territorial waters, a well-camouflaged "civilian fishing boat" carried a team of Navy divers. Their mission: search for any trace of the reconnaissance jet that had gone down.

The large-scale search-rescue operation utilized sophisticated sonar and depth-finding equipment that should have been easily capable of tracing the outline of a sunken aircraft. But the extensive operation thus far had been a waste of time. The rear admiral in command had signaled in his considered opinion that the plane wreckage was nowhere in this vicinity.

It was a strange one, all right. A real puzzle.

What happened to that missing recon plane?

Something weird and as yet unaccountable, for sure. The plane's systems data stream, routinely monitored by the *Carl Vinson*, had detected a weird anomaly indicating the plane's equipment was functioning normally. . .*but extreme heat was registered coming from outside the fuselage!* That's all that was known. The data transfer had broken off at that point.

The "civilian fishing boat" had done a subsurface sonar sweep per the admiral's orders, issued despite his personal opinion that the operation would likely yield nothing. The brass wanted "every inch of that plane's last reported position covered".

The boat's sensors had detected something far below its present location.

Ron Spargo was one of the divers.

Ron loved the sea, a feeling he attributed to having been born and raised in Hawaii. Growing up on Maui, he'd spent at least half his young life in the water. His father was a world champion surfer. Ron had started surfing when he was eleven. Before joining the Navy he'd been a pearl diver back home, putting himself through college working summers as a cliff diver to entertain the tourists. Ron Spargo even loved seafood more than any other cuisine! His mother, considered by many to be the greatest cook on the island, was said to have as many seafood recipes as there were fish in the sea.

His parents had ingrained in him a sense of responsibility along with the philosophy that if you love what you do to make a living, it will never seem like work. He'd liked the sound of that the first time he heard it and that outlook had served him well. As a Navy diver, there was always a challenge to be met and it was always underwater, Ron Spargo's favorite environment. For Ron, it didn't get any better than serving your country by doing something you love to do.

Today was no exception.

After launching himself from the boat in sequence with the others, he'd executed a forward semi-roll and dived straight down. The scuba suit he wore, a Deep Diving System with an alloy helmet that featured a closed-circuit rebreather unit, eliminated the need for compressed air canisters, enhancing underwater movement. The helmet featured sophisticated microchip circuitry for ultrasonic transmission and reception, facilitating underwater verbal communication between the divers and with their surface vessel.

He swam with his arms close to his sides, pedaling hard with both fins. His eyes had no trouble getting accustomed to the wavering sunlight that filtered down to these depths. A school of fish fled at his approach. At a distance, in various directions, the other divers swam about. Sporadic snippets of exchange crackled through his helmet with crystal clarity.

The watery world was alive with fish, a continually changing pattern of bright colors.

Ron was permitting himself to luxuriate at a sensory level in this underwater kingdom. Had he been a civilian and lucky to have himself an inexhaustible bank account, he'd have gladly spent whatever it took for a deep-sea diving expedition to the South China Sea. And here he was, doing just that. How sweet could it get?

His depth gauge read one hundred. One hundred-fifty. One-seventy. Two hundred feet. At each level he swam about, conducting a methodical visual search of his surroundings.

The voice of Russell, the group's ranking Master Diver came crisply across the tacnet.

"Got it! Here it is, boys!"

Ron and the other divers could see him giving them arm signals to come join him. Along with the others, Ron propelled himself in that direction as fast as his legs could thrash.

A vertical and jagged rocky outcrop extended from where its base reached down into the bottomless sea darkness. At this depth the filtered light was dimmer but Ron and the other divers now clearly saw Russell pointing to where the outcrop had blocked their view.

And there it was.

Wedged against the far side of the rocky outcrop was a misshapen mass of metal that only vaguely resembled an airplane, as if the plane had somehow been melting and the process was interrupted when it plunged into the water and sank.

Ron Spargo's mother and father were deeply religious and had raised him in the Catholic faith. To Ron, the barely recognizable remains of a fuselage and the stubs from either side that had been wings, and the silvery glow of filtered sunlight upon it, more than a little reminded him of a crude silver crucifix shining its light down here in the watery depths.

There was a brief exchange, the men roundly congratulating Russell and expressing satisfaction that their mission was a success. Russell communicated news of their find to the surface vessel.

Strangely, there was no response from above.

It was difficult to read expressions behind the diving masks but Ron did note that the divers' eyes mirrored his own confusion. Must be a technical glitch.

Russell voiced the same thought.

"Something's wrong topside. Let's check it out."

Curiosity, anticipation and concern combined within Ron during their ascent, and he knew every one of his dive teammates felt the same way. A break in communications from the surface was unusual enough to raise concern, although a minor tech bug could not be ruled out. Seemed like the more high tech the world became, the easier it was for one little microchip to screw everything up. The surface vessel might not even know they'd lost contact.

The brief decompression stops dictated by their individual software every hundred feet or so was especially frustrating, though necessary. Each decompression stop allowed time for a diver's body to readjust to the demands of water pressure; gas moved out of the tissues, back to the lungs. Ron and the others continued to move closer to the surface between each decompression stop.

After the second of two one-minute stops, something strange began to happen, commented on across the tacnet by Russell and the others. But no one seemed to have an explanation. With their ascent nearing the surface. . . *the water began growing warmer. Warmer than usual. . .*

When the bottom of their surface vessel was almost close enough to touch, the water became *hot.* Very, *very hot.*

Ron had a brief memory flash of the time Mom and Dad took him and his sister on a three-hour hike to a remote, secluded hot springs on Maui. Until now, that had been the hottest water he'd ever known.

Those were his final thoughts.

When the divers reached the surface, the ocean was literally *boiling!* They became part of a world gone insane. The last thing Ron heard was his and their dying screams of agony.

God, the screaming!

Those in the water were boiled alive. The fishing boat became a blur. On its deck where sailors should be assisting the divers in boarding, unrecognizable horrors that were human beings in uniform wailed an ungodly cacophony. Their uniforms crumpled. *The men within the uniforms were melting!*

None were alive to hear the deafening thunderclap of the explosion that vaporized everything. The water continued to steam for several minutes until the South China Sea again became placid.

Smooth as polished glass.

Seated at his submarine's command console, Admiral Yang's thin lips curved into a smile without humor.

Another successful application of Dragonfire. . .

CHAPTER 10

From the air, Hong Kong is beautiful.

Cody's seat aboard the passenger jet afforded him a bird's eye perspective of the island as the commercial airliner banked in for its final approach.

Hong Kong. The name translates as Fragrant Harbor. For centuries, situated at the mouth of the Pearl River, it's known as the Pearl of the Orient. A small island, eleven miles long and less than five miles wide, with a population of over one million people. Communities hug the shores, and then climb into the high hills.

Victoria Harbour, ringed by mountains, was even busier than he remembered. The harbor was crowded as always with an infinite variety of modern vessels and traditional Asian craft; fishing boats and exotic Chinese junks with great elegant sails alongside junks with dirty, torn sails. Brand new naval vessels steamed past tiny sampans. Giant ocean liners were interspersed with cargo-heavy freighters, scampering ferry boats and an endless array of miscellaneous small craft.

Then the jet was touching down at Kowloon's Kai Tak Airport where the runways thrust out from the peninsula into the waters of Kowloon Bay. Kowloon was where most of the major hotels were located.

The Washington-to-Los Angeles leg of the journey had been a fast three-hour hop hitched aboard an F-35 Lightning II, courtesy of the Air Force. Then, on the sixteen-hour LA to Hong Kong flight, Cody had invested ten hours in a restful, deep sleep, mercifully free of those torturous, knife-in-the-psyche nightmares that had become so common. He dreamt nearly every night of the family he'd lost. Even in the heat of action when there was only focus for the job, there was the subliminal constant that this would be the mission when he pushed it too far, succeeding in the mission objective and yet somehow also finally achieving his physical death; paying the blood debt for failing to protect his family. And then, then at last he would be reunited with them. This time he awoke on the flight refreshed and invigorated, free of any trace of jet lag.

He deplaned with the rest of the passengers. It had been decided that his insertion into Hong Kong should be low key, especially after the probable loss of Phil Hagan in Canton. Unarmed, Cody had settled into First Class as a mid-level suit working for an American electronics firm that manufactured its components in China.

He always expected trouble and complications on a mission. Here in Hong Kong, though, he would not yet have to deal with the severe in-your-face police state hassles he would soon encounter on the mainland.

Politically and culturally, Hong Kong found itself in a unique position following the Chinese government resuming its sovereignty over the island in 1997 after more than 150 years of British colonial rule. The catch was that Beijing designated Hong Kong a Special Administrative Region of the People's Republic of China, which meant Hong Kong's system of government was separate from that of mainland China. A peculiar and interesting arrangement. China granted the region a high degree of autonomy to preserve its economic and social systems for fifty years from the date of the handover, resulting in a rambunctious local economy where Chinese communism wrestled with Western commercialism. Citizens of the island overwhelmingly identified themselves as natives of Hong Kong rather than as Chinese.

Cody, with only a carry-on travel bag slung over his shoulder, navigated Customs without difficulty.

A young woman, fresh-faced in her mid-twenties,

approached him. She wore her blonde hair in a stylish shoulder-length cut that framed healthy, unlined features in a most flattering way. She wore a crisp white blouse and a sensible black pants suit that did not conceal a trim figure.

She started to speak.

Cody said, "You're here to meet me."

A statement, not a question.

She nodded, extending a hand.

"Beth Conroy, Mister Cody. I'm from the embassy. I'll be your handler."

Brisk. Self-assured. Pretty blue eyes with a cute smattering of freckles across her nose.

Cody said, "Next time use the public address system. That way everyone can hear you."

She bit her lower lip, a blush touching her cheeks. She pitched her voice so low, he could hardly hear her.

"Oh gosh, I'm sorry."

He sidestepped her and strode on at a brisk pace.

Hong Kong is cosmopolitan—most people understand English—and yet at its heart is an ancient, timeless place as unchanging as the soul of China itself. The fragments of conversations he overheard around them were mostly in the singsong Cantonese dialect. The vast majority of the island's population was Cantonese; a hard-working people known for their good cheer and strong sense of humor. The most innocuous conversation in Cantonese could sound to a foreigner's ears as if the speakers were engaged in a deadly disagreement.

No harm had been done.

She hurried to keep up. They made their way along an arcade of gift shops and restaurants. She was practically jogging to keep up with him.

Cody said, "Be honest now. Is someone using you to play a joke on me?"

She frowned.

"I'm, uh, I'm not sure I know what you mean."

"Did Sara put you up to this?"

"I don't know anyone named Sara."

That rang true enough. She wouldn't, considering the need to know firewalls that were SOP in an operation like this.

"I can see you're displeased," she said. "Maybe we should start by getting a few things straight."

"Maybe we should. Why aren't you off skateboarding or something?"

Her blue eyes grew frosty.

"What the hell is that supposed to mean?" When they'd gone another dozen paces without him responding, she added, "We do have to work together, you know. Civility would make it a lot easier. I've read your file, Cody. I've heard about your loss. I mean, I read about it in your file. I want you to know how-"

"Stop. Don't say it."

"Well, I am sorry. And while it's true that I'm new

to my post, I can assure you I am not inexperienced with regards to administrative procedure. Don't think of me as your handler if that doesn't work for you. Consider me a resource, okay? Frankly from what I've heard, I didn't expect this to be easy."

She softened that with a conciliatory smile.

They exited the terminal onto a paved area that fronted an extended drop-off/pickup zone, busy accommodating people and vehicles. After breathing nothing but recycled airplane air and the air-conditioning of the terminal, it renewed Cody further to inhale the real thing. The air was warm and silky. He recalled that Hong Kong humidity never let up, day or night.

He said, "Okay, here it is. I'm not interested in what you've heard. I don't have time to spare. Give me what you know." He leaned in close and said for her ears alone, "I need my gun and I want to see Missus Kwan."

"Then you're talking to the right person." She indicated the expansive parking lot opposite the loading zone. "I'm parked over here."

As they walked, Cody considered the situation.

She was a nice kid. Raised by good folks who'd instilled confidence in her; maybe irksome brothers so she'd grown up accustomed to male ways. Not easily intimidated. A good sign.

He'd observed over the years that the women he encountered in his line of work, professionals at every level of the espionage bureaucracy, were invariably exemplary in the performance of their duties. He encountered dedicated, highly motivated men too, naturally, but the world being the way it was, the women had to work and push harder, had to prove more, to get to where they were.

That was Beth Conroy.

He would have preferred someone with more seasoning. Someone older. Inexperience could get an experienced man killed, or anyone else for that matter. He would keep an eye on her both for her protection and to watch for her mistakes so as not to be undermined by them.

But his first impression?

She was okay.

Not that he intended to make it easy for her! That would not be doing her any favors.

"So," she said with a smile that a younger man would have found charming, "do you think we can work together?"

Cody said with an off-hand shrug, "We'll see. Sometimes a man has to make do with the tools at hand."

CHAPTER 11

Her car was a sensible silver Mazda3. She went straight to the driver's side.

Cody generally preferred to drive but he was not a nervous passenger. On this initial run into the city from the airport, he could take more in. He could always command the steering wheel if necessary. For now, it was all good.

In the car she handed him the packet that had made it over from DC ahead of him, in a diplomatic pouch: his Beretta M9. He relaxed somewhat, as much as he ever relaxed, once he was again armed.

And they were off!

Beth exhibited acceptable urban driving skills allowing Cody to maintain a vigilant eyeing of their backtrack and of the street scenes passing by: a raucous, over-amped metropolitan three ring circus of rickshaw coolies hustling their way between double

decker buses, taxicabs and trade vehicles. A boisterous atmosphere permeated the streets, noisy with an
intense, industrious air. They passed a scene of rev-
elers parading with firecrackers, celebrating a wed-
ding; a procession of colorful ceremonial dragons.

When he was satisfied that no one was following
them, Cody said, "So where is Missus Kwan?"

"She's in one of the safe houses we maintain in
Hong Kong. It's maintained by a dissident named
Ling Pao. He and his wife were waiting for Yuki
Kwan when she was delivered on schedule by a boat
man named Chua."

"Chua. He's the Triad connection?"

Beth nodded. She winced as the Mazda narrowly
missed clipping a rickshaw.

"Hagan has used him several times. I wasn't crazy
about it either but you find your assets where you can,
right? Utilizing a well-established pipeline, with the
payoffs already in place up and down the line, out-
weighed the negatives of using him."

"Where is he now?"

"I don't know. He hasn't been heard from since we
lost contact with Phil Hagan."

"Can you say double-cross?"

"The possibility has been considered of course,"
she said. "But what would the Triad gain by double
crossing the CIA?"

"Who the hell knows? Not knowing that doesn't

rule them out. Does Chua know about this safe house you're taking me to?"

"Of course not."

"Let's hope you're right. Tell me about Ling Pao. How well do you have the dissident underground wired?"

"Hong Kong is the base for opposition to the government," she told him. "An active center for the underground."

"I read the intel briefs on the flight over," said Cody. "What do you have that didn't make the briefs?"

A double-decker bus cut in front of the Mazda3. Beth steered them into a lane of oncoming traffic just long enough to pass the bus by goosing the accelerator. She was forced to abruptly decrease speed to avoid rear ending a motorized rickshaw. They continued on.

She said, "Ling Pao's group is close to networking all the major southern cities online to national markets which, to a large degree, will make it even more difficult for Beijing to close the country off."

"Anything else I should know from between the lines?"

"There's this. It came in while you were in transit. The Hong Kong station has received a heads up that there's a Chinese government assassin—code name Nightwind—who's been assigned by Beijing to disrupt the Canton-Hong Kong pipeline."

"Disrupt, not shut down," Cody noted. "Makes

sense they'd try and if the pipelines have been in business this long, who knows how many threads they could find to follow."

Beth said, "That's what happened to Hagan then."

"Not necessarily," said Cody. "There are too many factions that want Doctor Kwan and Dragonfire, whatever the hell that is. Hagan's either a prisoner or he's dead. Anything else and he would have been resourceful enough to get word back to you. He's gone. It's this guy Chua that I want to know about. Maybe he died with Hagan. If the Chinese have him, he's singing his head off. If Chua is free and operating, that could be trouble for us. You ran a search on Nightwind? Gender? MO?"

"It's a common enough combination of words but in this context it's new to us." She started working the Mazda's brake pedal. She said, "Here we are."

Ling Pao's establishment was a modest two-level structure on one of the busy streets of the Central District. The small storefront was sandwiched in between an arts and crafts store on one side and an herbalist on the other.

The street was lined with shop signs in huge, colorful Chinese characters. Gaudily outfitted tourists rubbed shoulders with women doing the family shopping who were dressed in the standard garb of drab cotton jackets and trousers, some with small children tied upon their backs while they made their rounds.

Multicolored laundry hung from bamboo poles out of windows. Young men rode bicycles, and everyone dodged and made way for the motorized rickshaws. An old fortuneteller stood on a street corner, chanting, advertising her services. A double-decker bus negotiated the boisterous atmosphere.

Ling Pao's shop was a sober contrast to these surroundings. Beneath the Chinese characters a small sign read in English: *Computers & Electronic Equipment Import & Export.*

Beth parked at a curb opposite and several doors down from the small store. They left the car, crossed the busy street and made their way along the crowded sidewalk.

The storefront was dark. The business entrance was locked.

Beth stood against the plate glass window and, using a hand held up to either side of her face as blinders, she looked inside. Then she stepped away from the window and turned to face Cody with a puzzled expression marring her pretty features.

"This is unusual. They're never closed during business hours. Ling Pao always has someone working the counter and sales floor. Something's wrong."

She was already angling double-time toward the mouth of an alley one building down. This time it was Cody who managed to keep up with her determined stride.

They left behind the hubbub of the street. The stench and sounds of an urban alley are universal. There was that closed-in feeling of a canyon of towering walls, the stink in dumpsters and the smell of urine fouling the air. The alley was noisy with the sounds of nearby traffic and yet there was a sense of isolation as if one step removed from the rest of the world.

They strode down the alley, Beth exuding a sense of urgency that prompted Cody to unleather his Beretta.

"Are you armed?" he asked.

She dipped a hand into her shoulder-slung purse and extracted a 9mm pistol.

They rounded a corner and advanced on a rear entrance to the computer shop. There was no one in sight.

Beth said, "Ling Pao and his wife live above the shop. They have a spare bedroom since their daughter got married and moved out. We brought Missus Kwan here and have been waiting for her husband to arrive."

She had a key for the back door.

Cody kept his Beretta up and in a two-handed grip, watching not only their back track but the roofs of the buildings that formed the alley. Something was wrong. The mission was already turning to shit and he was only an hour in-country.

They entered the building by the numbers, like a practiced team, Cody grateful for her training which belied her innocent manner and appearance. When the door was unlocked, she covered him while Cody went in. No one opened fire on them. Cody then covered the short, narrow hallway while Beth joined him. Walled by storage cabinets, the passageway led to a stairs leading up and the shop beyond.

The interior of the building was still. Street noise was a low, muted mumble.

They advanced past the stairway, pausing where the passage gave way onto the display room and counter area that occupied the front two-thirds of this level.

Overhead fluorescents had been turned off, cloaking the display in a shroud of chilly gloom. The layout could have been transplanted from any shopping mall back in the States. Rather than the busy, intensely Chinese ambience of the street scene outside, in here were orderly rows of computers and electronic parts with labels and price tags in both languages.

The three bodies were sprawled in an aisle shielded from the front window by shelves displaying printers. Two of the dead were young men in their twenties. They had collapsed onto each other, indicating they'd been made to kneel, and then executed with one round to the back of the head. The young woman must have sprinted away when the violence erupted, before a third bullet to the back of the head stopped her. Blood had pooled around their heads and congealed on the otherwise spotless tile floor.

Cody touched the back of his fingers to the flesh of the nearest dead man.

He said, "Stone cold."

A quiet sound snapped up his eyes and his weapon. He lowered the pistol.

Beth knelt near the woman's body at the end of the aisle. She was retching. It didn't last long. There was a sink behind the counter. Beth went to it, rinsed her mouth out, dabbing cool water to her temples. When she turned to face Cody her color had paled but her eyes were clear.

She said, "Ling Pao's daughter. She worked here for the family."

"The men?"

"Nephews, I think. But where—"

Cody lifted a finger to his lips, indicating silence.

"Maybe upstairs," he whispered, "and maybe not alone."

She nodded her understanding. Her color was returning by the second.

Together they withdrew from there, retracing their steps soundlessly to the stairs that led up to the living quarters. Again covering each other, they cautiously ascended.

They found the bodies in the master bedroom.

Ling Pao and his wife, who looked to have been in their sixties, had been told to lie face down, side by side upon their bed. They'd been executed, each with a single bullet to the back of the head.

Cody and Beth were the only living beings in the building.

They lowered their weapons. Cody was ready for Beth to again yield to being overwhelmed by the bloody horror they'd walked into. He wouldn't blame her or hold it against her. Beth Conroy just hadn't seen enough butchered bodies yet in her career. But she held it together. She was tough enough.

Cody said, "Three shooters at least. One to keep watch. One to handle the staff downstairs. One to come up here for Missus Kwan," he nodded at the remains on the bed, "and to do this."

Beth said, "Nightwind?"

He considered that.

"A hit team from Beijing? Maybe. Maybe they've got Kwan and they want to use his wife to keep him in line. But I don't think she's dead. Someone took her from here to bargain with. This crime is home-grown."

"The Triad."

Cody nodded.

"Way it was explained to me, the 10K Triad wants Dragonfire too. That's the game and Yuki Kwan is the pawn. Hagan's river friend, Chua, either knew where they were taking her before they left from Canton or he followed Missus Kwan here after he brought her to Hong Kong."

Beth stared with sad eyes at the two corpses on the blood-soaked bed.

"They were good folks. She loved to cook and would listen to anyone's troubles with a sympathetic ear. All Ling Pao needed to be happy were his computers and his woman. And all they ever wanted together was to make the world a better place. What happened here. . .Cody, it shouldn't go unpunished."

"I'll take care of that," said Cody. "We're proceeding from the assumption that the local Triad boss has her."

"Yu Cheng. But I don't understand. Missus Kwan would never go willingly. And all of these murders. . .why did it draw no one's attention?"

"Professionals were at work," said Cody. "Silencers. There won't be any fingerprints. No one in the neighborhood will have noticed anything strange."

"What about the ones who were killed? They were docile and simply allowed it to happen?"

"Most civilians would be intimidated by the sudden appearance of an armed intruder taking command," said Cody. "They wouldn't respond offensively. They didn't have the training or the weapons. The ones downstairs were made docile by a reassurance that nothing bad would happen. The shooter who did this," he nodded to the corpses on the bed, "only had to threaten Missus Kwan. Pack your bags and come with us, she was told, and everyone will be spared."

"She was traveling light," said Beth. "There's no trace here of what I saw her bring in."

"The third team member stood with her outside in the alley while the other two finished the job so there'd be no witnesses. Missus Kwan may not even be aware that they were killed. The team melted into the surroundings the same way they came with Missus Kwan as their hostage and it was done. No one saw or heard a thing."

"I've heard stories of the Triad assassins," said Beth. "I thought they were legends."

"The legends are true," said Cody. "They managed to execute a woman in the States who was being held in federal custody."

Sirens pierced the air with a strident immediacy.

"The police," Beth said. "What will we tell them?"

"Now I know you're pulling my leg," said Cody, holstering the Beretta under his jacket. "We're not telling them a damn thing because we're not going to be here when they show up. Come on. Let's get the hell out of here."

CHAPTER 12

When they reached the parked Mazda, Cody took the wheel and drove them away from the crowded street of shops. Before they'd gone a quarter mile, he observed in the Mazda's rearview mirror that they were being followed.

His attention to surroundings, heightened since his jet had touched down at Kai Tak, was yielding results. The fact that he was being followed at any given point, no matter where he was or what he was involved in was hardly baseless paranoia. He habitually practiced counter-surveillance techniques, the residue of a lifetime devoted to covert ops. It essentially meant remaining constantly attuned to every nuance of one's immediate surroundings, be it seated at a table in a restaurant or as now, on a crowded thruway on foreign soil.

Traffic flew bumper-to-bumper at a high rate of

speed but remained orderly without a whole lot of lane changing, making it easier for Cody to note the white Fiat, with a dent in its right front fender, shifting lanes with him as he angled for an upcoming exit.

Beth regarded him, noting Cody's fixation on his rearview mirrors, inside and out.

"What is it?"

"White Fiat," he said. "Pacing us. Shifting lanes whenever we do."

She glanced into her outside rearview.

"How do you read it?"

"The hit team left a spotter behind. Tidy. No loose ends. Keeping an eye on the place after the hit team was gone. When we showed up, getting us stalled out in a police investigation was too good an opportunity for them to pass up so they called the cops."

He shifted lanes for an upcoming exit. The Fiat joined the traffic flow behind the Mazda3, maintaining a four car-length trailing position. Cody passed the exit, and instead took the next one. The Fiat never lost position, also exiting the freeway.

Beth said, "What are you going to do? Engage?"

"I would if it was the hit team," said Cody, "but it's not. After a mass wipeout like what went down at Ling Pao's, the team has gone underground to whatever hole they came out of. The spotter is an expendable from the lowest rung. He or she won't know squat."

"But what if you're wrong?"

"Our mission," said Cody, "is Missus Kwan. She's not in that car. Anything else, including that Fiat behind us, is only a distraction. She's wherever Yu Cheng has her."

She studied him with open curiosity.

"So what are you going to do?"

"Watch."

Things got progressively difficult for the Fiat driver.

Plotting out his course thanks to the Mazda's GPS, Cody drove straight to an open market district; multitudes of pedestrians, noisy motorcycles, honking buses and cars. He exercised additional basic evasion maneuvers and soon lost the tail. They returned to the freeway. While keeping an eye on the traffic flow he passed the next three exits before taking an off-ramp. This time he drove a zigzag route through residential neighborhoods, satisfying himself that he'd lost the Fiat.

Cody continued driving without any particular destination in mind for the moment. They traveled through a section dominated by only the very best department stores, subway stations and flashing neon signs. Then came the financial district. Hong Kong was a dense city of sharp contrast. Old and new. East and West. Modern business buildings stood side by side with tiny shops offering the products of ancient arts. Neon signs of every imaginable shape, size and color, in English as well as Chinese, flickered brightly, jumping and whirling everywhere.

Cody said, "Tell me about Yu Cheng."

"Mind if I smoke?"

Cody cocked an eyebrow.

"I didn't think you smoked."

"I don't. I mean, I haven't in two-and-a-half years." She withdrew a single cigarette and a lighter from her purse. "I've carried this damn butt with me all that time to prove to myself how strong I am; that I could resist."

"Light up if you have to."

She did, exhaling the first lungful of smoke, with a small cough, directed through her side window which was open a crack.

She said, "How do you deal with it, Cody? You saw what I saw back there at Ling Pao's. How do you cope with something. . .something like *that*? Have you become numb to it?"

"Save the psychology," he said. "Right now direct action is called for."

"Sorry but I mean, come on! Five people were just snuffed out as if their lives meant nothing." She took another drag on the cigarette and blew another stream of smoke out the window. Her fingers holding the cigarette were steady. "Direct action sounds good. What you want to know about Yu Cheng?"

Cody said, "Yu Cheng has Missus Kwan. He wants Dragonfire. Keeping her under wraps will turn a profit for him on the deal no matter how it goes down. But are we sure he's our man?"

"He has to be," said Beth. "Yu Cheng is an Incense Master, which makes him a ranking member in the organization. They've expanded their operations in France, Spain, Germany, even in mainland China. But there's growing factional violence among the Triads. It's getting out of control because no dragonhead has risen to unite and govern worldwide. Being based out of Hong Kong, Yu Cheng is closer to the power base than anyone."

"All right, you've convinced me," said Cody. "Yu Cheng is our man. Given the situation, where would we be likely to find him?"

Beth took a final drag on her cigarette. She flipped its remains, half-smoked, out the window. She made a face.

"That tasted like shit. I think I've given up smoking for good."

"Yu Cheng," said Cody.

She withdrew a cell phone from her purse.

"Encrypted," she said, gesturing with the phone. "We've had Yu Cheng under twenty-four hour surveillance since Hagan made his Triad connection." She began texting. "Come to find out the Triad smuggles goods and people *into* China as well as out. Bosses have been known to seek cover and lose themselves on the mainland when the Hong Kong cops stage one of their crackdowns."

"You have a man on Yu Cheng?"

"A woman, embedded in his organization. The

Triad uses legitimate business as a front for laundering money, just like the Mob back home. We secured her a position in one of those legitimate fronts. From there she was able to hack into Yu's private email account. There should be traffic after what happened at Ling Pao's. There." She sent the text.

"We get a fix on Yu Cheng," said Cody, "and me and him are going to have us a serious chat."

"Getting to him won't be easy," said Beth. "He has layers of top-end security."

"Nothing is going to stop me," said Cody. "But here's the thing. What happened at Ling Pao's, there's more of that coming. I need to sideline you and find my own transportation."

"Wait a minute, wait a minute," she said. "Do I strike you as someone who quits halfway in?"

"I'm trying to look out for you."

"I've been trained to look out for myself. Am I in, Cody? Remember, I am a resource."

Dusk was coming on. Night would be one more complication, added danger to what he must do in Hong Kong tonight. Beth knew the score. She was worthy and yes, he *could* use backup.

He said, "When it gets heavy, don't say I didn't warn you."

Her cell phone pinged.

"Okay, here we go," she said. "It's my contact. She'll have something."

CHAPTER 13

Beijing, China...

In a Politburo conference room, two elderly men sat behind a large table.

Captain Lim Wei stood at attention before them, his cap under his left arm. Captain Lim was in his mid-thirties. His uniform was smartly pressed. He had been hastily summoned to this meeting with no briefing on what to expect.

Lim was fully aware that he was in the presence of supreme power.

The three men wore identical green uniforms that bore no insignia of rank. All insignia had long ago been abolished from The People's Liberation Army except for a single red star. Each man's cap was before him on the highly polished table. Opposite the bay window was a wall to wall mural of a young, dynamic

Mao Tse-tung leading a column of youthful soldiers on the Long March, pointing the way against a backdrop of snowcapped mountains.

Beyond the large bay window on the top floor of the Great Hall of the People, dull gray sunlight shone down over the one hundred acres of Tiananmen Square. Water from the previous night's rain, in scattered pools across the flagstone, reflected the gloomy light and the ornate incandescent streetlamps like mirrors of steel beneath the low, foreboding sky. Orderly throngs of bicyclists and pedestrians hurried about their business, overseen by the towering portrait of Chairman Mao mounted above the Forbidden City's Gate of Heavenly Harmony.

Defense Minister Huang, one of the men behind the table, commenced the meeting with a prolonged coughing fit, soiling a white kerchief with traces of scarlet. In his seventies, Huang was-thin boned with a shock of white hair above a narrow face. When the coughing ceased, he stared at Lim with steel-cold eyes that belied his quavering voice.

"Captain Lim, would you not say that China's greatest threat to stability has often come from within?"

Lim nodded and spoke promptly. He wanted to impress.

"No theme recurs more frequently in our history," he said, "than the drive to preserve our unity." He spoke in a measured cadence of respect. "The epic of our dynasties is punctuated throughout by warlords clashing for power."

This elicited a small smile from old Huang.

"It is good that you understand our history, Captain," he said, "for then you understand the crisis facing our great nation today. The last dynasty was cowed by European and Japanese expansionism, and ever since we have been at odds with forces beyond our borders. Yet today, much as in the day of the warlords, there is the clash of power from within for control of the People's Republic."

He was referring to the simmering, persistent undercurrent of rumor, heard in the upper echelons of power, concerning an imminent coup by hardline forces within the military.

As Minister of National Defense, Huang took orders only from the Chairman himself. The man seated beside him was General Boa, Chief of Staff of the Army; the nations ranking officer responsible for military movements and operations. Lim had been wondering about the reason behind his being summoned here. Now he knew.

If there is a coup, he thought, *these two old tigers and the Chairman, at the pinnacle of power, will be the first to fall. They're worried. They're desperate. They want something. . .*

General Bao was near Huang's age but in considerably better physical condition. He also studied Lim closely.

He said, "You have been most thorough, Captain, in your efforts to locate Doctor Kwan."

Lim acknowledged this with a curt nod.

"I only wish I could report satisfactory progress."

"What is your latest information?"

"We're following up leads in and around Canton. Something will turn up. Anti-government sentiment is deeply embedded down in that area despite the vigorous efforts of Major Zhao."

Huang cleared his throat. He leaned forward in his chair.

"What do you know about General Kwan?"

Lim prided himself on possessing an orderly mind and a precise nature. As an investigator, he never missed a thing. But the question caught him off guard.

"Doctor Kwan's brother? We monitor the general's mail and telephones. He is cooperating completely. As yet there's no indication of any contact between the general and the doctor."

"What is your personal opinion of General Kwan?" asked Bao. "You may speak freely."

Lim chose his words carefully.

"Until I was assigned to track down his brother, I knew of the general only by his considerable rep-utation. He came in for an interview at my request. He was cooperative, yet vague. By his own account the general and his brother have not spoken in years. This was confirmed by the information contained in their individual security clearance files."

"And what was your impression of the general as a man when he sat before you for the interview?"

"General Kwan is a Marxist conservative," said Lim. "He played a leading role in quashing the 1989 Tiananmen Square demonstrations. He has not mellowed with age."

Huang said, "Captain, returning to Doctor Kwan. Has your investigation uncovered any suggestion that the doctor has aligned himself with a possible coup?"

"*Doctor* Kwan?" Lim emphasized the title to make sure there was no doubt which Kwan brother he was talking about. "Like many men of science, Doctor Kwan has shown a distinct lack of interest in politics. He has no interest in overthrowing the Chinese government."

Huang's blue-veined hands became fists.

"He would prefer to see the Dragonfire project delivered into the hands of those who would use it against us! Severe penalties await Doctor Kwan upon his return." There was brittle anger in the old man's voice. "He would have a weapon of this magnitude placed under the stewardship of the United States. This must be prevented at all cost."

General Bao raised a hand as if to calm the naked rancor in Huang's words.

"It is *General* Kwan who has come to our attention," he explained to Lim. "Remarks have been overheard. He associates with officers of his rank whom we suspect of plotting against us. The discontent that festers within the military is what drives the coup. Hardliners would see us drastically scale back China's economic growth. They think our socialist ideals are being chipped away and destroyed by our policies. They see China's increasing economic ties to the West as undermining our national focus. *You* don't believe that, do you, Captain?"

Lim's response was again prompt. Automatic.

"Definitely not!"

"Good." Bao leaned back in his chair, pyramiding his fingers beneath his chin. "You will broaden the scope of your investigation to include General Kwan not only as the doctor's brother but as a possible lead to identifying other coup plotters."

"I will see to it," Lim assured them.

"The general is presently in Canton," said Huang. "He flew there aboard a military jet this morning. His family is from a fishing village not far from there. You referred a moment ago to Major Zhao. Zhao's provincial command provides the general with a personal security force when he visits. The fact is, the general has been consolidating his sphere of influence to the other branches such as our Air Force and Navy for some time. He and Admiral Yang have grown particularly close, communicating on an almost daily basis. We only recently become aware of this."

Lim said, "May I be permitted a question?"

Bao nodded.

"Speak."

"What of the Americans? I should deploy immediately to Canton. The general is there. Doctor Kwan is likely there. What should I expect? But surely the US has undertaken an operation to get to Doctor Kwan."

Huang snorted his displeasure.

"The thing gets darker and more tangled with every passing second! Let us not forget the Triad, curse their dark souls. General Bao has seen to the details. At this juncture, I can only offer wisdom. Mind this as you proceed: to trust is to sign your death warrant."

General Bao said, "The Americans had a man in Canton but chances are he's dead, which means they're sending someone else. We need to determine where General Kwan stands, and you need to locate Doctor Kwan before Dragonfire falls into the hands of our enemies."

"Those are your orders," said Huang, "You are dismissed."

Lim rendered them a smart salute. He about-faced and departed.

How strange, he was thinking. *These old men, weakened by age, fiercely devoted to guiding China into its future versus younger, more virile men—would that include General Kwan?—committed with equal fervor to upholding the past.*

Whichever side won, it would be a fight to the death. . .

CHAPTER 14

They'd blindfolded Dr. Kwan for so long, he'd almost become accustomed to it. He was seated alone in the rear of a moving vehicle. Shackled, hands and feet. Ankles and wrists, more precisely. Though he could not see, he knew there would be a man, armed with a rifle, seated before him, next to the driver.

He'd been roughly shuffled between vehicles and anonymous buildings—in and out and out and in again—so many times he'd lost count. Sometimes shoved with a painful jab in the kidneys from a rifle-bearing guard. His importance and value to his captors was apparent, as was their utter disregard for his comfort and personal dignity as a human being.

The vehicle slowed. The driver swung into a turn.

Dr. Kwan allowed his weary body to be swayed by centrifugal force this way and that on the seat. The driver continued applying the brakes. They had been traveling at a brisk speed for... his mind stumbled.

How long had it been since they'd clasped the shackles on him?

Time no longer mattered.

At one point he had been taken into a building where there was a tomb-like silence. Their footfalls echoed along a corridor. He was shoved into a room.

He'd managed to remove his blindfold. He was in a plain room, nothing on the walls. He heard nothing and so assumed the room was soundproofed. He could have been in downtown Canton. He could have been on the moon. There was a bucket. He relieved himself. There was a cot upon which he reclined. A high-wattage overhead light in a wire mesh resulted in a suspended semi-conscious state that was partly sleep, mostly not, for he didn't know how long.

He had found himself lapsing into nostalgic reverie; a way the mind had of dealing with psychic stress. He likely idealized his childhood. The world of the young boy he was. Were the skies always as blue as he remembered? An only child. Idyllic days before his brother was born. Free run of the small fishing village where generations of his bloodline had eked out a living from the sea. Beaches where he would gaze out across an infinity of blue ocean and somehow understand that anything was possible. Then a shadow morphed into the dreams of half-sleep. The shadow assumed a shape that could only be his brother materializing into the world. An ominous shadow that foretold the end of innocence. . .

Soldiers with rifles had thundered, or so it seemed, into the room, interrupting the dream. Rousting him roughly awake. The blindfold replaced, he was again prodded with rifles and rude commands. That was hours ago. Hours? No! Days. Days had passed since that night in Canton! Another night in another place. Always under heavy guard. Fed only rice and water. From now until the day he died, he would be a prisoner. Freedom had been so close!

He had so compartmentalized the idea of capture that it had come to seem an improbability. An abstract that was thought about less and less as he'd prepared for the journey from Canton to Hong Kong. His treatment at the hands of his government would be harsh. The only question now was how long it would be before he was sentenced to the prison camps or worse for his treason. He wondered why he hadn't already been handed over to higher authorities and made a public spectacle of. Apparently, this initial detainment was only a taste of what was to come now that they had him.

The vehicle came to a stop.

The driver climbed out and held open a rear door of the vehicle. Reaching in, he grabbed Dr. Kwan by the arm, drawing the prisoner from the vehicle.

Dr. Kwan stood with his feet planted firmly on the ground, weakened but steady. The soldier still held him by an arm. Even blindfolded Dr. Kwan knew the second soldier and his rifle would be positioned nearby. He drew a deep breath of morning air. The sunshine warmed him pleasantly. Sunshine! It was a new day.

A new day in hell.

Bootfalls approached.

Kwan thought, *This is what it must be like to be blind; to picture what is happening because you hear it clearly but not knowing if you're right!* It bred paranoid apprehension, making his throat dry.

"Was there any trouble?"

He recognized the voice. He'd last heard it on that dark pier in Canton. . .

The soldier with a grip on Dr. Kwan's arm said, "No, sir. The prisoner caused no trouble."

"Release him. The good doctor is not going anywhere." Zhao walked up to Kwan. He removed the blindfold with one snap of his wrist. "You see, Doctor? There is nowhere for you to go."

The first thing to draw Kwan's attention was the vivid red birthmark that covered a third of Zhao's face. It appeared even redder in the sunlight. Zhao's eyes glittered like those of a snake.

They stood before the Headquarters Building of the provincial military base, a drab collection of brick buildings surrounding a parade ground. There seemed to be considerable activity around a row of armored personnel carriers.

Dr. Kwan had wondered if he'd ever see the commandant again. And here Zhao stood, reigniting the vivid memory of Zhao escorting him away from that scene of men lined up beneath the high intensity lights, facing the line of armed soldiers. From that point, he'd been blindfolded and the shuffling reality of being moved about began.

But what of the ones left behind?

Had it been the chatter of gunfire that he heard—or thought he heard—after he'd been blindfolded and trundled into a vehicle and whisked away? In his heart he knew it was gunfire. Once he was led away, the soldiers had opened fire. Those men grouped with Hagan at the end of the pier had gone down under a hail of bullets.

And the young woman from the university commune who helped in providing shelter and transit? It shamed him that he could not recall her boyfriend's name with everything else that was happening but he did remember the girl's name. Mei Chan. Had she too fallen under the volley of rifle fire?

Now more than ever, Dr. Kwan was grateful that his Yuki was safe in Hong Kong.

He said, "Major Zhao, when will I be formally charged?"

Zhao snickered as if the question was not worthy of a response.

"This way, Doctor. I have someone who wishes to

speak with you...alone."

He led the way into the headquarters building. One of the soldiers poked Kwan cruelly in the kidneys with the muzzle of his rifle to urge him along.

Feeling weaker by the second, Dr. Kwan trailed Zhao into the building with the soldiers behind him, their rifles covering him every step of the way. To complain or resist would only goad them into further abuse.

Zhao evidenced a thin patina of self-control but beneath it he shared with his men a streak of uncouth cruelty. For many peasants, the People's Liberation Army provided the only avenue to acquiring skills and prestige but most of them never lost the core of primitive savagery of their lives before military service.

Dr. Kwan considered the significance of the fact that he was no longer blindfolded. Unlike previous stopovers, their footfalls did not echo through deserted corridors. It was not the middle of the night. They were not secreting him in an anonymous pit.

Uniformed personnel, male and female, hustled between offices and along hallways, exuding a sense of bureaucratic purpose, pausing only when he and his guards passed. His captors wanted him to know that he was in their headquarters. He was supposed to be impressed. But he was too fatigued in mind, body and spirit at this point to be impressed by much of anything or anyone.

Zhao stopped at a closed door deep in the heart of the administrative labyrinth. He opened the door and stood aside. Both soldiers put their palms against Dr. Kwan's frail back and gave him a shove that sent him stumbling in.

He expected them to do more and so was surprised when he turned to find the door slamming shut. He didn't bother checking the door. It would be locked from the outside with the soldiers posted as sentries. There was no other way in or out of a small, simple room furnished with only a scarred rough table and a matching chair to either side. An interrogation room.

Dr. Kwan sank into the chair facing the door. There was nothing to do now but wait. He would not have to wait long. *So close to freedom but now they had him! There was no escape.*

He'd spent his life rising above this level of base survival. His study of physics had brought him into a social stratum of highly developed intellects and ideals. This sort of harsh, menacing reality—guns, locked doors, a complete lack of kindness—was more suited to his brother, General Kwan. Dr. Kwan's life was his work, always engaging and challenging. His personal life was built around a lovely, intelligent wife who doted on him ("great men need looking after, darling") with the best life had to offer in food, music and physical comfort.

When he needed to draw back and recharge from

stress, there was his favorite book, the ancient *Tao Te Ching*, to dip into; to guide him through those times of personal challenge. Lao-tzu's eighty-one short verses comprised a profound discourse on the nature of existence; over the centuries translated more than any volume in the world except the Bible.

Dr. Kwan concentrated on the rhythm of his breathing, willing his heartbeat to stabilize. How could the teachings of a man like Lao-tzu possibly matter or be of value today after what the world had become, ruled by savages like those who now held him?

Legend said the author of the *Tao Te Ching* was a keeper of the Imperial archives in ancient China. Despairing of the continual bloodshed during a period of warring states, the old man decided to ride westward on his donkey into the desert. It is said that at Hanku Pass a gatekeeper, knowing of Lao-tzu's reputation for being a man of wisdom, begged him to record the essence of his teaching. Much like the Christian Biblical scripture, the guidance for a serene and productive life had been translated and handed down for thousands of years. Simple truths, profound in their simplicity. In dwelling, be close to the land. In meditation, go deep in the heart. In dealing with others, be gentle and kind. And yet in modern times Lao-tsu along with the Buddha and Confucius, had been largely erased from the public consciousness in China by a government that regarded all religion as a public opiate. These policies were enforced by the military in which his brother served.

Sitting there, waiting for he knew not what, it came to Dr. Kwan that the relevance today of those ancient teachings was traceable to its very beginnings. The original was first conceived in reaction to violent conflict. The struggle is eternal. The light embraced by Dr. Kwan versus the darkness embodied by men like Major Zhao. But as time marched on, the names of the warlords faded into dust along with their bones while the wisdom of Lao-tzu lived on.

The thought of Zhao interrupted the epiphany of his meditation.

Footsteps approached in the corridor outside. A key turned in the lock.

How long had he been sitting in this interrogation room? They had relieved him of his watch that first night. Minutes? Hours? Did it matter? What did they have in store for him? Lao-tzu could help him deal with the past and the present. . .but what about the future?

Dr. Kwan braced himself inwardly.

Remember this, whatever happens, he told himself. *Yuki is safe. Whatever my fate, they cannot hurt her.*

The door swung inward.

And Dr. Kwan found himself staring with wide eyes at someone he had never wanted to see again.

CHAPTER 15

Cody stood on the rocky outcrop and looked down upon the lights of Deep Water Bay, sparkling far below him like diamonds scattered across black velvet.

0230 hrs.

Hong Kong is a crowded urban environment—skyscrapers, glitz and hustle—but there are isolated areas where the natural backdrop has been preserved. The southern shore is one such area.

Reputed to be the wealthiest neighborhood on earth, three streets in the Deep Water Bay community are home to nineteen of the city's richest residents with an aggregate net worth of $123 billion. The most exclusive residential area of Hong Kong, all of the properties in Deep Water Bay are owned by billionaires.

One of those properties—a mile and a half downrange from where he stood, along a secluded side street that branched off Island Road—looked like a medieval castle in the greenish glow of Cody's Night Vision binoculars: a sprawling multi-level affair of winged, tiled roofs, balconies and turrets hidden behind high, thick walls. Armed sentries were visible. A stronghold set into a hilly slope. Gardens flanked east and west, the west side with a lotus pond, fountains and patio. A main gate, set into a corner of the wall, was heavily manned.

In a word: impregnable.

The owner: Yu Cheng, the Boss of Bosses of the Hong Kong's 10K Triad.

Beth Conroy's contact in the legitimate front organization run by Yu had reported that she'd hacked abnormally high email traffic, coded but obviously indicating major activity centralized at the Yu residence. Previously established routine surveillance of the property confirmed a spike in backup security arriving.

The Triad boss was going hard. Something big was going down. And that "something big" in this context could only be the murder of five people and the kidnapping of Mrs. Yuki Kwan.

The outcrop of rock upon which Cody stood was near the summit of Shouson Hill. At his feet, a sheer cliff wall dropped straight down to rocky rubble hundreds of feet below. At this elevation a breeze cooled the warm night by several degrees. Overhead the universe was a black dome of stars, the myriad of twinkling lights clear and bright from up here on this secluded piece of ground, removed from the crowded city.

Cody drew back several yards from the ledge. Due to the wingsuit he wore, his movements were ungainly, inhibited like someone walking underwater.

The wingsuit he and Beth managed to acquire—which had taken some doing, given the hour—was of the tri-wing design: three individual ram-air wings of black fabric attached under the arms and between the legs.

Beth Conroy had proven to be a worthy resource. With the political juice of the US embassy behind her, a reliable outfitter had been found. Valuable time was then spent on preparation and logistics. When she'd made a point of questioning the risk involved, Cody had not bothered to mention that not long before, he had been going up the side of a supertanker during a night storm in the middle of the Pacific. Why explain anything to anybody? He welcomed the risk.

Wingsuit diving had become an international fad in recent years. It involved skydiving from airplanes, land formations and, in the case of urban enthusiasts, from man-made structures like bridges and skyscrapers, and riding the thermal air currents. The modern wingsuit adds surface area to the human body, enabling a significant increase in lift. It's designed for safety though Base Jumping, the term for what Cody was about to undertake, was one of the most dangerous sports on Earth. The fatality rate was one in 500, with a far higher number of sustained serious injuries.

Cody had learned wingsuit diving as a civilian leisure-time activity. It was an exhilarating experience. With more than two hundred skydiving jumps to his record in both military and civilian life, he'd come to relish the unfettered sensation of personal freedom. He loved yielding to friendly air currents, physical instinct and an understanding of the principles of flight. The natural born thrill seeker in him had enjoyed mastering the challenge.

That was before he lost Carol and the kids...

The application of that leisure-time pursuit to this mission became apparent once he'd determined the impregnable nature of Yu Cheng's fortress.

He securely adjusted his Night Vision Device goggles. He took a deep breath and took off at an awkward run, straight for the ledge where he flung himself out into empty space into a vertical drop using the forces of gravity to accelerate, generating the airspeed necessary for the wingsuit to function and generate lift. For a short time, he was dropping like a rock. Gaining speed. Plummeting down *down* down! The air rushed by. The lights of Deep Water Bay raced up toward him.

Then he adroitly directed his fall, achieving a sustained glide, altering both his forward speed and descent by manipulating flight characteristics such as changing the shape of his torso, arching and rolling the shoulders and moving his hips and knees, altering the amount of tension applied to the suit's fabric wings. Awkward and cumbersome as the wingsuit was on land, upon becoming airborne the fabric instantly melded as one with the wearer, not unlike a second skin, the black wingsuit rendering him virtually invisible against the night sky.

Seconds after leaping from the ledge, Cody was advancing through the darkness—*flying!*—at 65 mph just meters above the terrain. Flying that low, he experienced an even greater sense of speed due to having such a close visual reference thanks to the NVD goggles, more than a little helpful in avoiding the hazards of proximity flying such as trees, rocks and shifts in the ground configuration hurtling by beneath him.

The difficulty of his approach was timing deployment of his wingsuit's parachute while steering toward the target in a controlled landing: the roof of the main house. The flight itself was a mere ninety seconds and seemed to go by in no time at all. He misjudged his approach slightly, guiding himself in as best he could, angling for the roof but ending up coming in feet-first into the back of a rifle-bearing sentry posted on a top floor balcony.

The sentry, caught completely off guard, was pitched forward, dropping his weapon and nearly falling off the balcony before righting himself and whirling about. A look of disbelief flared across his features, stalling him for a vital second when he beheld the black-suited figure in the weirdest getup imaginable, like some alien arrived from outer space.

The "alien" was on the guy before the stunned sentry could regain his senses or his rifle. Suddenly the apparition was bracing him to the balcony, a knee pressing painfully upon his throat.

Cody said, "Do you speak English?"

The guy sputtered frantic Chinese. Mean eyes in a pockmarked face.

"Wrong answer," said Cody.

With his knee increasing pressure on the guy's throat, he tightened a hand to either side of the man's head and started to squeeze and twist.

The sentry was aware enough to understand that if he made too much noise, he would surely die. His words came as a ragged whisper.

"No! I speak English! Don't kill me!"

"Where is she?"

Facing death, the reply was muttered without hesitation.

"Next flight down. . .bedroom. . .north end of house."

"Right answer," said Cody.

And he killed the guy with a sharp twist that broke the sentry's neck.

The image of those five murdered souls was burned into his mind. People like that deserved to live. Not filth like this. Yu Cheng's sentries were more than likely the same crew that had been dispatched to grab the Kwan woman and nullify Ling Pao's safe house. Killing punks like this was like taking out the trash.

He shucked the wingsuit and discarded the NVD goggles. He didn't like having to leave this valuable equipment behind but there was no choice in the matter and maybe it would be recovered if his actions resulted into a police raid on this fortress.

The wingsuit and the goggles had gotten him in. As for getting out? Improvisation was the name of that game.

He wore black, from knit cap to boots, beneath the wingsuit. He drew the Beretta and considered his options. Bedroom on the north end of the house? That could suggest anything. Prisoner. . .or willing guest? This was no time to be naïve or make assumptions. Anything was possible. The only way to know was a look-see.

This presented two options: leave the balcony, enter the house through a bedroom that was visible beyond a closed sliding glass door and from there advance on to where the woman supposedly was. Or he could likely reach the north end of the house by an exterior approach. The medieval architecture of the façade sported a narrow shelf of masonry across its length. It could well accommodate his traversing the distance between a balcony at the north end of the structure and the balcony where he stood.

A roving foot patrol and a number of posted sentries about the grounds were visible from Cody's vantage point. It was a good bet none of them would find a reason to look up, and even then his black garb would make him hard to see. Weighing that against the likelihood of having to confront a security presence inside the house, it was no contest.

He stepped onto the balcony railing and from there it was an easy lift to position himself on the narrow shelf. With the Beretta in one hand, using the other hand to balance himself against the wall behind him, he carefully made his way along the shelf toward the next balcony where a light had just gone on behind its curtained glass door.

CHAPTER 16

Cody gained the balcony at the north end of the house.

The sliding glass door had been left open about six inches. A man's voice could be heard speaking from inside the bedroom. Speaking in Chinese, the voice pitched in a conversational tone but with a sinister edge just beneath the surface. A mild cajoling voice but that sinister undertone implied a subtle threat.

There was no response to the man's voice.

Was the guy talking to himself?

Cody didn't think so. He took a position next to the glass door on the balcony, his index finger curved around the Beretta's trigger. He chanced risking one eye to peer around the doorframe, just enough to see between the frame and wispy white curtains.

Soft lighting bathed a low-ceiling bedroom. Elegantly furnished with Chinese draperies and art objects. Cody's nostrils caught a trace of incense.

Two people in the room.

A man and a woman.

The man was about fifty years old. Handsome with the stocky, bullish build of the Northern Chinese, wearing, a belted burgundy smoking jacket, woven with a gold dragon design, over pale blue pajamas. The slippers were Gucci.

The woman, Chinese, was tied spread-eagle upon the bed, each wrist and ankle lashed to a post of the four poster bed.

Cody recalled the photographs of Mr. and Mrs. Kwan in their respective files. The physicist was elderly, not frail but showing his age. Cody had noted the three decade disparity in age between husband and wife but the photos of Mrs. Kwan conveyed not a hot token spouse but a matronly type, modest and retiring, anything but glamorous. Timid, mousy; attentive as a mother or older sister to the needs of her brilliant husband.

The woman, whose body was stretched taut upon the bed, was Yuki Kwan. No doubt about that. Her sculpted Eurasian features, the beauty of which she'd never be able to truly conceal, belonged to the woman in the photos, yes. But everything else. . .not so much.

She had wide cheek bones and long greenish eyes. The natural golden tan of her skin was exquisitely smooth, a golden bronze, nude except for a lacy black push-up bra and a pair of matching thong panties. At five-five and maybe 110 pounds, she was the perfect embodiment of feminine beauty except for the fierce resistance in her eyes and the obscenity of her bondage.

The man was leaning over her, caressing the jet black hair that fell onto her bare shoulders. His coarse thumb ground brusquely across full lips, pouty now with the gasping shortness of her breathing. She was struggling against her bonds but could not avoid his touch. There was cruel amusement in whatever he was murmuring close to her ear.

Cody chose that moment to make his entrance, sliding aside the glass door, the Beretta held down against his outer thigh.

He said, "Is this a private party or can anyone join?"

The man drew himself up and stepped away from the bed, turning to face Cody, not in startled surprise but with centered calm and a powerful grace. He said something, coolly and almost nonchalantly in Chinese.

"English," said Cody.

The man said in the same tone of voice, "Do you know who I am?"

"From here you look like an over the hill Casanova resorting to desperate measures." Cody indicated the woman on the bed. "Turn her loose."

Yu Cheng said, "Why bother? You are already a dead man, sir, whoever you are. After they have carried your body out," he indicated the woman on the bed, "I will return to this."

Cody extended the Beretta with a straight-armed aim between the guy's eyes.

He said, "Cut her loose."

The moment held, but only for a moment.

Yu gave his right arm a shake. A jewel-handled dagger with a long, wicked-looking blade, in a sheath up the sleeve of his smoking jacket, slid into his right hand.. He spoke with a smirk.

"I was merely inquiring as to whether Missus Kwan had reconsidered my offer of hospitality."

Cody never shifted the Beretta's bead on Yu Cheng as the Triad boss went from corner to corner of the bed, freeing the woman of her bonds with a series of surgical swipes with the blade.

Cody said, "Now drop the shank."

Yu was in the process of stepping away from the bed. There was nothing threatening in his body language. He simply half turned and flung the dagger at Cody with blinding speed and accuracy.

The blade would have sunk into Cody's heart if he hadn't been expecting something. Yu hadn't clawed his way to the top of a mob of killers by being soft and folding easily. Quick as he was in raising the dagger to throw it, his speed was matched in Cody's response. Cody drew sideways. The dagger sailed past him, missing by mere inches. Its point sank into the wall behind him, the jeweled handle quivering.

Cody had to make sure.

He asked her, "Who are you?"

Freed, she swung perfectly shaped legs around and sat up on the bed, massaging her wrists.

"Who the hell do you think I am?" She stared fire at Yu Cheng. "Your hospitality," she sneered. Loathing dripped from her every word. "You think I would share your bed? Never!"

She went directly to a closet. Inside was a travel bag, apparently hers, thrown in there after Yu's men had stripped her and tied her down. She went about throwing on clothes from the bag; probably the outfit she'd been wearing when she was taken from Ling Pao's. The street clothes belied the lady's spicy taste in undies. She didn't quite look like a dowdy peasant. She'd adopted an everyday drabness in appearance, camouflaging her stunning natural beauty.

While she was getting dressed, Yu Cheng regarded Cody. The Triad boss appeared relaxed, projecting smug, arrogant confidence.

"Mind telling me what you intend to do?"

"The lady and I are leaving," said Cody. Unless you want to tell me what happened to Doctor Kwan."

Yu Chen sniggered. He nodded at Yuki.

"If I knew where Doctor Kwan was, would I waste my time baiting a trap with this morsel?"

"What about Chua?"

"I know of no one by that name."

"And I suppose it wouldn't do any good at all to ask you about the murder of Missus Qian while she was in government custody."

Yu registered a hint of mild amusement.

"I am unfamiliar with the case but some people, it would appear, know too much to live."

Yuki, now fully dressed, whirled angrily to face them.

"Kill him!" she snarled at Cody. "Kill the pig. He is walking evil!"

Cody said, "I have a better use for him."

"Ah, you are an intelligent man." He spoke warmly as if in genuine sympathy with another's predicament. "Yes, whoever you are, do the right thing. You have me under the gun. What harm can I do?"

"Don't listen to him," hissed Yuki, a note of desperation in her plea. "Kill him, I say!"

Yu's smile was one of pure indulgence.

"Follow your conscience, round eyes. Turn me over to the authorities. Yes, that's the idea whatever your complaint."

His every word dripped with mocking superiority.

"What are you waiting for?" Yuki demanded with heightening desperation. "*Do it!* Destroy him while we have the chance!"

"I told you," said Cody. "He has a use. Grab your bag if you want it. We're out of here."

Yu Cheng gave a soft sigh as if bored with some minor distraction.

"Enough."

He lifted his voice and called out a one-word command in Chinese.

In response the bedroom door burst open automatically, powered inward by a broad-shouldered, bald-headed security guy who took in the tableau before him with a glance: his boss under the gun of a strange intruder. He pawed for a sidearm, whipping the piece up with lightning speed.

Cody shifted his aim and squeezed off a quick shot.

The bullet took the bodyguard high in the chest and kicked him over like a hammer blow to the floor. There was lots of blood.

Gunsmoke hazed lazily in the air.

Yu Cheng glanced from the corpse on the floor up to Cody. He didn't look overly alarmed.

"I think we can forget about trespassing," he said coolly. "That was murder."

CHAPTER 17

"That was self-defense," said Cody. "I forget, is kidnapping a capital offense in Hong Kong? Oh yeah, I remember now. It is. Yuki, were you brought here against your will?"

Yuki had crossed to work the dagger loose from where it was embedded in the wall. When she turned back to face them, she held the small traveling bag in her left hand, the dagger in her right. Pure hatred inflamed her eyes.

She snarled, "This is nothing but foolishness! Finish him," she urged Cody. She gestured with the dagger. Its blade glinted warmly in the intimate lighting. "Finish him or I will!"

A rumble of running, trampling feet could be heard in the hallway beyond the open doorway, advancing in a hurry.

Yu Cheng smirked.

"Save your breath, foolish wench," he told Yuki. "You have gained nothing. And you, sir, will tell me everything you know as you die by inches. No one will hear your screams. Did you know there are ways to make a man beg for death? You shall know what I mean before the sun rises."

Yuki made a sound that reminded Cody of a hissing alley cat. She surged at Yu Cheng with the dagger. Cody blocked her move, chopping down with his left hand to deflect her thrust before she could get in close to the gangster.

"No, you don't," he said. "This guy's our ticket out of here."

Yu Cheng started to smirk another smug comment.

Cody moved double-time fast, getting behind Yu Cheng. The Triad man uttered a very un-smug gasp of sheer surprise when Cody's left arm wrapped across his throat. He jerked Yu's head back sharply while, at the same time, he rammed two inches of the Beretta's barrel up Yu Cheng's rear end, pajamas and all.

"Now we walk out of here." Cody held the guy flush against him and was practically whispering in his ear. "And if one of your boys even looks like he wants to rock and roll, guess who gets it first where it hurts the most?" He gave the gun an extra nudge for emphasis. "Get me?"

The doorway became filled with the men Cody had evaded outside. They held automatic assault rifles. Their point man drew up short with a look of stunned disbelief at the sight of their top man's predicament. The sentries behind bumped into him, slapstick-style. The point man started chattering something in Chinese.

Cody nudged the Beretta, rougher this time.

"Executive decision time, Boss. Do you and I and the lady walk out of here or do you kiss life goodbye the hard way?"

Yu Cheng didn't miss a beat. He started spouting off to his men in Chinese. He switched to English after only a few words when Cody tightened the grip on his throat.

"Stop, men," Yu ordered. "Lower your weapons."

His voice was as calm as someone asking for a glass of water. A heartbeat passed while everyone held their breath in astonishment. In this world, the word of Yu Cheng was law.

The point man spoke over his shoulder, not taking his attention off the scene confronting them, still unable to believe his eyes.

"You heard Mister Yu. Everyone step aside and allow them to pass."

"Not good enough," said Cody. "I want every man here out of the way. They leave their guns."

"Go downstairs to the break room," Yu instructed them. "Wait for me down there. Let us pass. No one gets in our way."

Rifles and pistols were placed upon the threshold, reluctantly but obediently, and with uncertain backward glances the sentries traipsed back down the hall. The sound of their footfalls receded to nothing.

Cody said, "Car keys."

Yu Cheng was so humiliated, as Cody intended him to be, that he could not find his voice. He could only indicate, with a glowering nod, the dresser top which Yuki immediately inspected.

She snatched up the keys.

"Okay, Boss," said Cody. "Let's take a walk."

Yuki remained close to Cody.

Cody crab-walked Yu Cheng through the house, never once relinquishing the grip of his left arm across Yu's throat or removing the gun from its nesting place.

Yu Cheng proceeded, adhering to the course of least resistance. He was hardly in a position to do otherwise given that there was a gun shoved up his butt.

They stepped outside, into the night. It had started raining while Cody was inside; a warm, light drizzle.

A five-car garage was adjacent to the main house. The three of them made their way along the short walk to a side door of the garage. Yuki remained close to Cody. Yu Cheng continued to bear his disgrace in silence.

There was as yet no sign of the security force.

Cody didn't know how long that would last but did not give it more than another minute or two. Yu's men had been told to remain out of sight and orders were orders, sure. But these were seasoned, hungry mankillers, not obedient schoolchildren. So far he and Yuki had been lucky but he knew from experience that something was bound to go wrong any time now. . .

Inside the garage, with Yuki at his side, Cody thumbed the electronic key ring. He was satisfied to see the lights go on and the doors unlock on what he estimated to be the fastest set of wheels: a sleek white BMW luxury sports car. He stepped back from Yu Cheng, disengaging the Beretta from the gangster's backside. He gave Yu a shove.

"Hands on the hood," he instructed. "Assume the position."

Yu Cheng recognized the command and obeyed, both of his palms supporting him on the hood of the BMW. He leaned forward, his legs spread slightly. Cody kept him covered. This was when the gangster could try something. Cody opened the front passenger and was about to order Yu Cheng into the car.

Before he could, Yuki made her move.

With the grace of a dancer she inserted herself between Cody and the man leaning against the car. She came in swiftly behind Yu on his left side, bringing up the dagger in her right hand for a thrust that sunk the blade to the hilt into his side at an angle that penetrated his heart.

Yu Cheng gasped deeply. He rose to his full height.

The woman remained pressed against him. She gave several sharp twists to the dagger. It only took a handful of seconds, so fast that only one detail leapt out to register with Cody: Yuki's face was not twisted in the blood rage of a passionate kill. Her lovely features were almost serene.

Yu collapsed sideways against the vehicle. With blood gurgling from the side of his mouth, for the briefest moment his dying eyes met those of the woman who had killed him. Yuki spat in his face. The spittle mixed with his hemorrhaging blood.

She said, "Go to hell, pig."

Those were the last words Yu Cheng heard, if he heard them at all. His knees buckled. He pitched face-forward at her feet.

Yuki extracted the dagger from his body. She wiped the blood from the blade on his elegant smoking jacket. Then it disappeared into a pocket. She retrieved her travel bag.

She said, "He should have put me in a room and left me alone. He would defile me. I take that from no man."

"I can see that," said Cody. "Let's go."

They piled into the BMW.

Cody kicked the engine to life and raised the garage door by remote. He tromped the accelerator. It was like goosing a race horse. The sports car burned rubber, tearing out of the garage as if fired from a catapult.

The security men had sensed the house was empty and were coming out in search of their boss despite his orders to remain inside. In no time they found the boss's body on the concrete floor of the garage.

Cody's eyes flickered to his rearview mirror.

Saffron flashes of gunfire in their wake! The sounds lost beneath the climbing acceleration of the Beemer's getaway. Beside him, Yuki twisted around in her bucket seat. When she saw the flashes, she instinctually ducked then straightened when the bullets struck the vehicle without effect.

Despite everything, Cody couldn't help but shout out a laugh.

"Yu Cheng had himself a bulletproof sports car!"

Then the BMW fishtailed out of the driveway and tore away from there.

CHAPTER 18

"You saved my life and I do not even know your name."

"Cody. Jack Cody."

"Will they follow us?"

"They'll think about it," said Cody. "You kind of short-circuited things back there, taking out the big dog. Yeah, they'll likely send out a scout team. Whoever's running the team will make that call. He'll want to look good for whoever replaces the boss."

They were traveling a narrow, lightly traveled secondary stretch of road that would soon link up with the busy Island Road. The drizzling mist made the blacktop slippery.

Cody lost control of the BMW for maybe three or four seconds due to a hydrofoil effect. The sports car had extraordinary responses and he was quickly able to regain control. He did not slow down.

Yuki asked, "Where are we going?"

"We need to switch cars. You upped the stakes, killing him like you did. I was hoping to get some answers out of the guy. He ordered a mass murder today."

Her attractive features had remained neutral since killing a man a few minutes earlier. Now her expression darkened in the car's dash lights.

"Ling Pao?"

"And his wife and his daughter and two nephews."

She watched the night world passing by outside the speeding car and for a short while there was only the sound of the windshield wipers.

Then she said, "So sad. Their only sin was to show kindness to me. You asked Yu Cheng the important questions. My husband's whereabouts, and about the boatman, Chua. You saw what Yu Cheng had done had to me. I had to kill him."

"What's done is done," said Cody.

He'd decided that since his goal was to take out as many bad guys as possible in the quest for his own redemption, he could hardly fault her for eliminating a piece of garbage the world was better off without.

Yuki said, "It's good that we're changing vehicles. If they find us, they will kill us."

"They'll try."

Her eyes shifted to watch him drive.

"You do not fear death?"

"Not my own. But I'd just as soon nothing happened to you."

"Thank you for what you're doing. Your government sent you, yes?"

"Yes."

"I feel like I'm in a movie, the way you. . .the way you rescued me. What is your name?"

He told her.

"And this place where we will change vehicles, is it far?"

"We're here now," he said, wheeling the Beemer into a sharp right hand turn onto a narrow strip of gravel nearly impossible to discern by any passing motorist in the blackness of night unless you knew its exact location.

Cody doused the headlights and guided the BMW along the approach to a gravel parking lot adjacent to the trail head of a hiking path. Densely populated as Hong Kong was, specified areas like this one near Deep Water Bay were maintained as natural habitats for public use.

The BMW drew to a stop beside a silver Mazda3. The only vehicle in the parking lot, Beth's car was practically invisible in the moonless night. The misting had diminished, leaving the forested trailhead a silent, damp, claustrophobic place. The weather seemed to insulate the spot.

He had not known, going into Yu Cheng's, exactly what to expect or how he was going to withdraw. The hit on a Triad hardsite could well have been the blazing end he was looking for. Withdrawal would likely be by vehicle. That's all the strategy he'd had, except for the likely need of logistical support at a point along the ex-filtration track. Beth had recommended this spot a half-mile from Yu's residence.

She'd chosen well.

Beth and Yuki exchanged a brief hug of greeting, remaining reserved given the situation. Cody recalled that Beth had been present when the boatman, Chua, first brought Yuki to Hong Kong. He was relieved to see a bond of trust already established between Yuki and Beth. Little things like that on a mission made a big difference.

Cody briefed Beth on what had just gone down at Yu Cheng's, including the Triad gangster's fate at Yuki's hands.

On the road at the opposite end of the gravel strip, a convoy of three black SUVs raced by going full speed.

When she saw them, Yuki said, "They hunt for us!"

"Time to evac," said Cody, "before they realize we gave them the slip and they start doubling back. Beth, I need Yuki to sit in front with me."

He slid behind the Mazda's steering wheel, grateful for a team player like Beth who took the rear seat without comment. Yuki joined Cody in front.

She said, "But should not Beth ride here in front? It is her car, after all."

Her discernible accent made her words pleasantly

melodic; it was difficult to imagine her thrusting a knife into a man's heart.

Cody started the Mazda and slipped it into gear.

He told Yuki, "I understand how you feel safer carrying a knife. And after seeing what you can do with a knife, I feel safer having you where I can keep an eye on you."

She responded with a slight frown that did not mar her beauty.

"Believe me, Jack Cody, after what you've done for me tonight, you are the last person I would ever wish to harm." She twisted sideways in her bucket seat to include the back seat's occupant in their conversation. "Beth, I never saw anything like it. This man is without fear."

Cody felt Beth's eyes on him.

"He's damn sure a good guy to have on your side."

Cody could think of no response to a statement, that wasn't trite, so he said nothing. Let them think whatever they want. The adrenaline was still pumping through his veins. *I'm trying to kill myself and they think I'm without fear. What a world!*

The Mazda reached the end of the gravel strip. Cody switched on the headlights in preparation for rejoining the sparse traffic flow on the highway.

He said to Beth, "I need a destination."

She replied, "Island Road to Repulse Bay. The Free Water Marina. I programmed it into the GPS. I've got a lot to report, Cody. Things have been happening while you were busy rescuing Yuki."

"Let's hear it."

Beth was not one to warm the bench while others worked the court. She'd wanted something to do while awaiting Cody and so had followed his directive to shake the tree of the Hong Kong underworld and see what shook loose. The US Embassy had long ago organized a network of informants across the island, like the woman planted at Yu Cheng's business, at every level of known illegal and semi-legal activity.

Hong Kong is a busy place. Something is always, always happening. Since US interests were so deeply entwined these days with the world of Hong Kong business—both legal *and* shady—it only made sense to monitor the local scene as much as possible. Nice thing about it was: the informer network worked both ways, gathering and disseminating information.

Word had gone out to everyone everywhere on the shady side of Hong Kong, from the tourist haunts to the underbelly sex dives, from the penthouse financial office suites to cutthroat back alleyways along the waterfront. One thousand dollars American would be paid for information on the whereabouts of a boatman named Chua.

Yuki said, "Chua. The man who brought me from Canton?"

"The same," Beth nodded. "A thousand dollar shell-out gets a lot of attention in Hong Kong. I didn't hear *about* Chua. I heard *from* him. He called me."

Yuki asked, "Did he say anything about my husband?"

"No, I'm sorry, Yuki. It was a very brief conversation. I had the feeling he was looking over his shoulder the whole time, afraid someone was coming after him before we finished talking. Very paranoid."

Cody's knuckles turned white around the steering wheel.

"Where is he?"

"We're heading there now. He's been staying underground in Hong Kong but now he says he needs to get out fast. He says he can disappear easier on the mainland and he wants that thousand for traveling money."

"Are you sure it was Chua you were talking to?"

"Yes, it was him. And there's more. He's, uh, also hoping that you'll accompany him into China. Says you can protect him until he finds somewhere to dig in. I told him I'd pass along the message. He's waiting to hear from me."

Yuki said, "We must be very careful. We are not yet out of danger. Is not Chua one of the Triad?"

"There is that," Beth conceded. "What do you think, Cody? You saw tonight the way Yu Cheng lived. Chua is a down and dirty river rat hustler. Would there be a direct line of communication between them?"

"If Chua had something of vital importance, he could get word to the top. The fact that we don't know where Chua stands means we have to check him out."

"And if it's a trap?"

Cody held open the lapel of his jacket, displaying the Beretta in its shoulder holster. He patted the piece with his free hand.

"That's what this is for."

Beth's expression said she remained unconvinced.

"Chua was Hagan's ticket out too. We've written Hagan off, right? Then the only way Chua could have made it out is if he's a double agent."

"That is a possibility," Cody admitted. "And yeah, it's also possible that Chua is setting me up. Yu Cheng's people could have got through to him. They want Yuki back, and they'll want my blood for what I did to their boss. But things don't happen that fast. Yu's body is still warm. And he was still breathing when Chua was angling over the phone. My take is yeah, Chua sold out Missus Kwan. But he's small potatoes and now he's too hot after those five people got killed. The Triad would rather see Chua dead than have a living tie-in to those homicides walking around, and Chua knows it. One less river rat and who would know the difference or care? That's why he's desperate. That's why he wants out. And that's why I don't think it's a trap. I want to hear Chua's side of it."

He steered the Mazda off Island Road, onto one of

the Repulse Bay exits when the GPS informed him he was near the marina.

He said, "Beth, when we part ways here I'll likely be catching that boat ride with Chua. Get Yuki to a safe place, safer than the last, and I'll—"

"No!" said Yuki. Strident urgency made the word sharp as the point of a spear. "If you are going back into China, it is to find my husband, yes? You must take me with you. My place is at my husband's side. He should have left Canton with me but he worried for my safety, as you are doing now and look what happened. Please, Cody. Take me with you." She must have read the uncertainty in his eyes. She pressed on. "I know the students at the university where my husband and I stayed. The doctor and I should never have separated. We will find him together, Cody, you and I."

He pulled the Mazda over to the curb and braked to a stop a hundred yards short of the marina.

"That's not a good idea, Yuki. I just took you out of danger. Let's keep you out of danger. Beth, tell her it's not a good idea."

"What's good about any of this?" said Beth. "You're forgetting that we don't have a single lead on Doctor Kwan's current whereabouts, and he is the mission objective. And don't forget this Night Wind assassin Beijing decided to throw into the mix. Your orders are to exterminate him with extreme prejudice if he happens to show up, which is a good bet somewhere along the line. Mister, I'd say you've got your hands full of crap to deal with. You need backup and you've got to admit, Yuki does have a personal interest."

Yuki added, "If you are going to risk your life for my husband, would you expect less of me?"

Cody grunted. There were things he didn't know about Yuki Kwan but he liked her style and he liked her display of warrior spirit. There was no doubt she was handy with a dagger.

"Face it, Cody," said Beth, "you're going into China and you've acquired a traveling companion."

"And you're back to sounding more like an embassy handler than a resource. Okay. Be careful, Beth. Thanks for all the help. Get this guy Chua on the phone and tell him I'm here and ready to do business. Come on, Yuki. Let's go hear what the boatman has to say."

CHAPTER 19

The Island Marina was a ramshackle affair, well below the upscale, millionaire-level marinas that predominated along the coastline of Repulse Bay. Beyond the marina, Victoria Harbour was an almost psychedelic swirl of movement, light and sound. The hoot of horns and the rumble of 'round-the-clock water traffic created a raucous symphony beneath the black dome of night. The marina was a quiet corner of the world existing separate unto itself.

Chua's sampan floated peacefully at her mooring, its navigation lights providing illumination. As arranged, Chua stood waiting for them.

Yuki had slipped her arm through Cody's as they approached. Cody could feel her muscles moving stiffly. She had his arm almost in a lock and was walking as if her spine were a steel rod. But she didn't slacken their pace, and she held her head high.

Chua greeted them with a bow. A bland smile did not reach his crafty eyes.

"Ah, so nice to see you again, Madam Kwan. And you must be Mister Cody? Miss Conroy described you well. Please, step inside where we may have our privacy. There is much to be discussed, yes?"

"You could say that," said Cody. "Lead the way. And no funny stuff or I'll kill you."

Keep it simple and direct, that was the Cody way, it being necessary to impress on the guy where he stood in the scheme of things. Cody had dealt with hundreds of small time hustlers like Chua in operations around the world. They thought they were smart because thus far they'd managed to stay alive in the shark tank. Not to be trusted and there was no need to be friendly, especially when money was involved.

Yuki remained mute, sitting beside him in the tent-like shelter, attached to the sampan's flat deck, that served as a sparsely appointed living space. Many Chinese lived in sampans or junks in Victoria Harbor and the surrounding bays, usually supporting themselves by fishing or performing day labor on the wharves.

After declining the obligatory offer of tea, Cody got straight to business.

"I understand you need protection."

With an oily smile, Chua indicated Yuki with a deferential nod.

"And I understand that I may be of service in reuniting the nice lady with her husband."

"Who are you afraid of, Chua?"

The boatman replied with a vague shrug, "These are dangerous times. There is talk of a coup."

Yuki eyed him with unconcealed distrust.

"Where is my husband? What happened to him? You were supposed to bring him to Hong Kong once I was with Ling Pao."

"We found the bodies," said Cody. "It was a massacre. Someone set them up."

Chua's bland expression remained unfazed.

"Very dangerous times, yes. It is why I myself must be gone from this place. I do not know who to trust. It is why I made the call when I learned you Americans are offering money for information about me. Who better to tell you about me than me, eh?"

"All I want from you," said Cody, "is what you can tell me about Doctor Kwan and Phil Hagan."

"It pains me to say I know nothing about that. It is true Mister Hagan and I were at a pier in Canton. The doctor arrived with his handlers at the other end of the pier. My understanding was that they were young people, students from the university. Mister Hagan went to join them. Then there was much shouting and bright lights. That is all I know."

"Like hell," said Cody. "Finish the story, boat man. What happened to them, and how did you get from there to here?"

"There was gunfire," Chua confessed. "Like a firing squad. I had shoved off from the pier at the first sign of trouble. Soldiers fired after me, but I was far enough away to become lost in the river traffic and they must not have identified me for I made it to Hong Kong but on my own. I was most lucky to escape with my life."

"He is a coward," said Yuki to Cody. "He deserted my husband and your man. When they brought me out, Mister Hagan was waiting at the pier with this one like he said. The university students brought me to them. Mister Hagan said they would be using the same method to bring out my husband." She raised an accusing finger pointed directly at Chua. "He betrayed them."

"Dear lady, no," Chua protested, gesturing with both hands. "There is a military commander in Canton. Major Zhao. I warned Mister Hagan about Zhao that night in Canton. Zhao is cruel. A human monster. What happened was a trap set by the major. I was lucky to escape."

"Coward! Is my husband alive or dead?"

"I believe him to be alive," said Chua. "Madam Kwan, I know nothing but shame for my cowardice. My way when I am in the employ of Mister Hagan has been to act ignorant, but I know who Doctor Kwan is. A defector. The manhunt for him is broadcast every hour. He has disappeared. But you must consider this, dear madam. If your husband is that important, would they execute him at night on the waterfront? Never! There would be a trial. A public spectacle. No, dear lady, he is among the living." The boatman patted his chest. "Chua knows this in his heart."

"Just out of curiosity," said Cody, "where is your heart? There's the Triad. The Chinese government, Missus Kwan and her husband, that is to say the US government. Whose side are you on?"

Chua became almost apologetic.

"Why, whoever has the most money. Whoever I fear the most. It is the way I was raised and have lived my life. The way of the river. It is true, I am a coward. No more than a humble, lowly boatman doing his best to stay alive."

"That's about as honest a self-portrayal as I've ever heard," said Cody without irony. "But let's cut through the crap, shall we? I want a few more answers out of you before we go anywhere."

"But of course."

"Ling Pao."

"Ah. My heart weeps for them, for his wife and their daughter and the others."

"I said cut the crap. If you didn't finger them for Yu Cheng, who did?"

"I have no answer for that," said Chua. "As the top man, Yu Cheng has Hong Kong wired, is it not so? That Ling Pao ran a safe house and that Madam

Kwan was staying there is information that could have come to him by many ways."

"If you're not concerned with any of that, why are you so hot to get out of Dodge?"

A deprecating chuckle was nearly lost in the grime of Chua's beard.

"Quite frankly, Mister Cody, a man such as myself is prone to make enemies. They are not all necessarily connected to each other. I have, er, former friends who are displeased with me, let us say."

Yuki emitted a short, unpleasant expulsion of breath.

"A coward and a scoundrel, this one," she said to Cody. "He plays both ends against the middle. He is not to be trusted."

"We're not going to trust him," said Cody. "Chua, there's no money in this for you, only survival. You need to get in country. So do the lady and I, so we'll travel together. I'll cover your worthless ass as far as Canton. That's where you're taking us. From there you're on your own."

"As you wish," said Chua. "It will be my pleasure and privilege."

Cody had given this considerable thought prior to making the offer. Diesel trains regularly made the ninety-mile trip between Canton and Kowloon. But Cody's white face, even with all the necessary forged papers, would be under close scrutiny if he rode openly by public transportation especially with Mrs. Kwan. Such routes were heavily patrolled.

"One thing," said Cody. "Madam Kwan doesn't trust you and since she's made this trip with you once before, I'm inclined to give credence to her concern."

"And what is your concern, Mister Cody?"

"That you could be leading us into a trap. Could be for the Triad, could be for the Chinese army."

Chua did his best to look horrified.

"Perish the thought. My friends, I would never do such a thing! I wish only to serve."

"That's good. And you know what?" said Cody. "I'm personally not worried about that happening. Not even a little. Want to know why?"

"Why is that, Mister Cody?"

Cody unholstered the Beretta lightning fast. He pressed its muzzle to the bridge of Chua's nose.

"Because at the first sign of trouble, I mean at the very first indication that anything is less than perfect, well, I'm going to blow your brains all over this grubby little boat. Is that perfectly clear, my friend? No matter what happens, if I get the slightest wrong vibe. . .you are dead. We understand each other, right?"

Beads of sweat had pearled along Chua's hairline.

"But of course! It is not to worry! A guaranteed safe journey to Canton!"

Cody holstered his pistol.

"Great. Let's get started."

CHAPTER 20

It was Sara Durell's third visit to the White House. Her first to the Oval Office since Martin Harwood had assumed the presidency in the wake of his predecessor's debilitating stroke. She rode in a taxi to the rear of Blair House, where she walked the remainder of the way, ushered inside by the Secret Service, and led to the simple waiting room where she took a chair across from the president's secretary, a polite young woman who stayed busy at her desk.

Less than a minute later, an oak door swung open. Jim Corbett, the president's Chief of Staff, emerged in earnest conversation with a man Sara recognized as China's ambassador to the UN, followed by a concerned cluster of staff members, none of whom paid her any mind as they hurried past.

In her honest, no-bullshit moments of self-reflection, Sara generally thought of herself as really nothing more than a lowly grunt who'd been promoted above her skills. She always felt impressed and humbled when summoned to these lofty environs of political power.

She wondered if she would ever see action in the field again. She'd gone through Army Ranger training; sixty-one of the hardest days of her life. The failure rate was way over fifty percent. That was followed by Special Operations. Black ops. Riding topside in a .50-caliber machine gun turret on a point vehicle leading a convoy into hostile territory, scanning the road ahead for signs of ambush. Operating outside the budget process. Field promotions. Deep recon. Small-scale offensive actions in hostile, often politically sensitive environments.

And these days?

These days she lived in a condo complex that came with a Jacuzzi and its own gym. She wore clean clothes and drove a nice car. And she sent good men like Jack Cody out to do the dirty work.

She told herself not to think about the guy, and yet she was certain that Cody was the reason she'd been summoned to the inner sanctum of the president. The call had reached her less than ninety minutes ago. Previous visits here had been scheduled, routine. One of the raps on the current POTUS was that he was a stickler for protocol. The fact that this summons was on such short notice had her ready for anything.

Jim Corbett reappeared a few minutes later, minus the ambassador and staffers. He saw Sara and gave her his best professional smile along with a mild, gender-neutral handshake.

"Captain Durell, thanks for getting here so promptly."

"The traffic patterns were in my favor for once."

Then they were in the Oval Office.

The president was just reaching for a remote control, pointing the device at a flat screen TV mounted on the far wall. The screen was filled with a military correspondent for one of the news networks, standing in front of the Pentagon, delivering a dour-faced report. The president thumbed the remote. The screen went dark.

He said, "I guess we should be surprised we've been able to keep this thing under wraps as long as we have. What's it been, almost two days? That could be a record for something like this."

Sarcasm and frustration were heavy in his voice. He was speaking to Whit Jones, Director of the CIA, and the only other occupant in the office waiting for Sara and Corbett when they walked in.

Jones' ebony features mirrored the president's concern.

"Implementing DEFCON 3 and deploying an aircraft carrier strike group to the South China Sea is the sort of thing that gets people's attention," he commented dryly. He nodded a greeting to Sara. "Captain."

Sara's personal interaction with the Agency's Director had been minimal but impressive. Whit Jones had earned a high level of respect throughout Washington as a no-nonsense man of integrity.

"Sir."

The president said, "Welcome to the crisis du jour, Captain. And it's a doozy. Have a seat. The reason you're here is that with things coming to a head on several fronts the way they are, the Cody factor in this mix has become critical."

Sara, Jones and Corbett each took an armchair; a half-circle facing the president. Sara's mind was processing. *Cody! Of course. Why else, given her role in this?* DEF-CON 3. Yes, she'd heard it on her car radio during her drive to the White House. Every branch of the US military presently postured in an above-normal state of readiness. That was not good. *A couple more notches up the DEFCON meter would mean imminent military confrontation. . .war.*

"I'm here to contribute whatever I can, Mister President."

"We sent Cody in," said Harwood, "with a single and simple mission objective. Bring Doctor Kwan and his Dragonfire project over to our side. Problem is, the whole context of the mission is a foggy mess. It started with a recon plane spotting Chinese sub activity. We lost contact with the plane. Hell, we lost the plane and its pilots. And now we've lost contact with the dive team sent to find them. China disavows any knowledge of any of this. Their ambassador claims to be as mystified as we are."

"Maybe he is," said Corbett. "With a coup ready to blow up in their face at home, it doesn't seem likely they'd choose now to get belligerent with us."

Sara asked, "Has any direct linkage been established between Dragonfire and whatever happened at sea?"

"That's where Cody comes in," said the president. "It's why it would be nice to hear from him. The recon plane's monitored data recorded extraordinary heating malfunction caused by an outside source before we lost them. That ties in with what we know about Dragonfire and what it can do."

Corbett said, "So if not the Chinese, who? A third party?"

"We can cancel out the Hong Kong Triad," said Sara. "Cody communicates with me using an encrypted cell phone with a direct satellite uplink. I've received exactly two calls from him since this mission began, both of them in the past few hours. The first call was to request my assistance in preparation for a strike, the second was to report its success."

Whit Jones raised both eyebrows, visibly more impressed than skeptical.

"Define success," he said. "A Cody strike on the Triad in Hong Kong, eh?" He gave a dry chuckle. "Sounds like he's living up to his rep for a man who wants to get killed. Last brief I saw said they were holding Missus Kwan in a fortified location; some sort of power play."

"They're not holding her any longer," said Sara. "She's with Cody. They're sailing up the Pearl River on their way to Canton as we speak."

Jones frowned.

"What the hell? We risked everything getting that woman out of China. We lost Hagan. Did you direct Cody to take her along?"

"Certainly not," said Sara. "I pointed out the same thing to him. He considers her a valuable asset. She's already in contact with the university commune in Canton that Hagan worked with."

Corbett said, "You can call Cody, right?"

"I've texted and spoken to his voicemail," said Sara. "To my chagrin, he doesn't respond. He only calls when there's a specific need, apparently. I seriously doubt he even checks his messages."

"We knew he was a lone wolf cowboy when we sent him in," Corbett said with a sigh. "Doesn't mean we have to like it."

President Harwood was irritably tugging at an earlobe.

"So, if we rule out the Chinese government and the

Triad in all of this, who else is there? A third party?"

"The next logical suspect," said Jones, "would be whatever faction in the Chinese military is backing this coup that's got Beijing so antsy. The rebels getting their hands on Dragonfire would be everyone's worst nightmare."

"I hate to say it," said the president, "but that does make the most sense. When Doctor Kwan approached us, he said Dragonfire could be made operational but that it still needed work. Okay, let's run for now with the idea that it is the rebels who are causing us this trouble, while we keep our options open. If Cody locates Doctor Kwan, he'll find Dragonfire."

Corbett said without enthusiasm, "Unless Suicide Cody finally lives up to his name and loses the whole thing along with killing himself. . .leaving us with an unseen enemy possessing a terrible new weapon."

The president seemed to have visibly aged in the short time since Sara had been shown in.

He said, "A weapon like that in the hands of a hostile power would put world peace up for grabs. Do we have any leads whatsoever at this point?"

"There is one thing," said Sara. "It's in Doctor Kwan's bio file. He has a brother in China. A general in the army."

CHAPTER 21

The Communications Center in the Great Hall of the People was far below the street level of Tiananmen Square: a cluttered, concrete-walled room filled with masses of American-made communications gear. There was the hum of the equipment, a minimum of hushed conversation and no other sound except for the clicking of many fingertips across keyboards beneath rows of monitors.

During the Cold War, China and the United States had jointly operated a string of electronic intelligence-gathering stations along what had been the Soviet border. The stations were furnished with American equipment and Chinese technicians. Enormous quantities of that equipment had been diverted to this sub-basement, unknown to most of the thousands of people who daily worked in or visited the Great Hall.

General Bao stood with Defense Minister Huang near a wall dominated by a bank of world-time chronometers. Technicians tended the rows of equipment with the precision of ingrained routine.

"We were intercepting an enormous amount of US radio traffic," Huang told the Army Chief of Staff, "much of it corroborating what their president told our ambassador. A missing reconnaissance plane in the South China Sea. The subsequent unexplained loss of personnel sent to search for it. We had hoped the ambassador's visit would quell the Americans' concern but that has not been the case. They've escalated their military posture to DEFCON 3. We believe they've sent one of their nuclear submarines into the South China Sea."

The old general's eyes were sharp.

"You *believe*," he echoed with distaste. "What do you mean, we *were* monitoring the Americans?"

"Apparently they've shifted communications to an emergency frequency that so far we've been unable to break."

"I was not aware such a problem existed," said Bao. "Do we not have access to their satellite positioning?"

"We do but the transmissions are being circuited through one of their new satellites," Huang explained. "It alters transmitting frequencies in a random fashion every few seconds."

"Could this be an American trick?" Bao wondered

aloud. "A test of our response time? The Americans must be aware of our internal crisis."

"A possibility," Huang conceded, "but for their military escalation to DEFCON 3. Americans do not bluff."

"I too have troubling news," Bao told him. "A fragmentation of command is emerging at military posts across the country. Army, Air Force and Navy. As yet unsubstantiated troop movements that have not been authorized. Gaps in our own communications. I'm taking immediate steps to get to the bottom of it but so far without success."

"Troubling," said Huang. "You no doubt observed, upon your arrival, the growing crowds gathering in Tiananmen Square. An atmosphere of civilian unrest is spreading throughout the city."

"It's all connected, I tell you," said Bao. "The coup has begun. The Americans are poised for war. The future of China, not to mention our lives, will be decided within hours."

"That is so," said Huang. "But we are marshalling our resources as well. Doctor Kwan and his brother, the general, are somehow key to this. I feel it in my old bones. I have ordered a database search that we might find some indication of General Kwan's involvement and culpability."

Bao nodded his approval.

"It is good Captain Lim has been assigned to this.

He is our most capable investigator, is he not?"

"He is, and he will come through. We can expect a report from him at any time."

At the Public Security Bureau's provincial headquarters just outside Canton, Captain Lim tried to keep the incredulity he felt from his voice. He could not believe what he was hearing.

"You say Major Zhao has departed with the entire detachment?"

"Y-yes, sir." The stutter of hesitation in the young lieutenant's response clearly indicated extreme discomfort at this face-to-face encounter with a military investigator airlifted in straight from Beijing. The young officer added, "A convoy of troop carriers was requisitioned by the major only yesterday."

Lieutenant Toi was in his mid-twenties. A slim, intelligent-looking fellow. His uniform, pressed. Boots, spit shined. He was, he'd told Lim, the single remaining officer left behind by Major Zhao along with a handful of low-ranking enlisted men. In other words, until Lim's arrival, the lieutenant had been left in command of the entire base.

Lim had sensed that something was wrong here when his helicopter first touched down. He'd been to this base before. From that experience and from

Zhao's reputation as an overachieving, proactive commander, he had expected to find the post alive with activity; to be greeted at the helo pad by no less than Zhao himself. Instead, the base was practically deserted. Ghostly quiet in the sunshine. Hardly anyone in sight. The helicopter was the only sign of activity.

Lim had demanded an explanation of Toi when they met. During the flight from Beijing, he'd gone through the appropriate database for the past two days. He could recall seeing no such troop transport requisition from Major Zhao. But that was not Lieutenant *Toi's most stunning revelation!*

Lim said, "Tell me again about Doctor Kwan."

His mind was reeling, processing what the young lieutenant had told him. Lim's career had seen its ups and downs. Sometimes an investigation fell into place easily, seeming to solve itself while far more often, nothing but dogged routine procedure investigation was required. But this. . .this was an incredible masterstroke of good fortune! Lim saw nothing but promotion in his future once this complicated turmoil was over and done.

Toi was saying, "Doctor Kwan was held here for only a short time."

"But you knew who he was," pressed Lim. "You knew he was the missing physicist who was defecting?"

"Yes, sir. It was my understanding that he was being held here until his transfer to Beijing. He had his own cell. We have a block of cells for dealing with dissidents. Doctor Kwan was kept isolated but he was well treated."

"Did you personally discuss this with Major Zhao? Was he following orders from Beijing or acting on his own?"

Toi gulped loudly. He was perspiring freely.

"Sir, one does not 'discuss' with the major. His command here is absolute, as is his intolerance for dissension from subordinate officers such as myself. I can tell you this. After General Kwan arrived, it quickly became apparent to me that he was not only in command by virtue of his rank, but also that he was privy to things like the convoy of troop carriers. I overheard them discuss the matter. General Kwan processed the requisition."

"Overhear anything else of interest?"

"Not from Major Zhao, no sir. But when the general came with a four-man guard to remove his brother, I heard him say to Doctor Kwan that they would be going home."

"You overhear quite a lot."

"I find it prudent to pay attention, sir."

"This coup that General Kwan and Major Zhao appear to be part of," said Lim. "Need I ask, Lieutenant, where your loyalties lie?"

Toi drew himself smartly to attention.

"I am loyal, my captain. It is why I was ordered to stay behind by the Major. No fault has been found in the performance of my duties and yet he and I never quite got along, if you know what I mean?"

"The only thing I need to know, Lieutenant," said Lim, "is can I count on you? I'm on an important and dangerous mission."

"You can count on me, sir! I am at your service."

"Excellent. With what resources remain, I want you to concentrate on the local dissidents. There is much happening today, and they are an integral part of it."

"I will give it my best," Toi assured him with another loud, nervous gulp.

Lim could tell the young officer knew he was in over his head in this matter but there were no alternatives.

He said, "When General Kwan left here with his brother, did they leave with Major Zhao's convoy?"

"No, sir. They departed separately from the Major."

"And you heard the general say they were going home. That could have been a figure of speech. Did the general elaborate?"

"No, sir. I overhear much, not everything."

"The Kwans are from a small fishing village on the coast, not seventy kilometers from here," said Lim decisively. "Find me a vehicle, Lieutenant. The fastest

one available. You are now in command of this base.
I will also need a man to accompany me. I'm driving
straight to that fishing village, Lieutenant. I want to
take one of your men with me for backup. We'll be
there within the hour."

"Sir, if I may. The helicopter-"

"Would alert them before we arrived. No," said
Lim. "I will arrive unannounced. Hurry now. The
trail is hot and there is not a moment to spare."

Mei Chan quickly drew her head down. She inched
back when the military vehicle stormed through the
main gate.

Having positioned herself across the road from
the Public Security Bureau headquarters, she had
spent the previous sixty minutes stretched flat upon
the ground, her bicycle resting beside her at the edge
of an open field. The field behind her was alive with
birdsong and the crackling chatter of crickets. The
sunshine was comfortably warm.

The field had likely been cleared to provide base
security; an open field of fire. Dissidents were held
within the compound walls. Torture was not un-
common. The field of fire was intended to discourage
breakouts and rescue attempts. No one would survive
a sustained volley if caught in the open.

But they had not counted on a teenage girl, a university student, relaxing on this sunny day on a long bicycle ride. Base security appeared surprisingly lax from her vantage point. She'd observed the convoy leaving. Motionless when a helicopter landed and, since no one came looking for her, she assumed that she had not been seen by anyone in the helicopter.

And now, this Jeep-like vehicle bursting from the main gate as if expelled from the base by a giant invisible catapult. Skidding into a two-wheeled turn, tires left the pavement and then gained traction, spewing dirt. The vehicle rocketed off away from the city, not toward it. It was soon lost to her sight.

No further sign of activity was evident from across the road. It went back to being another quiet day in the suburbs of Guangzhou, which everyone Mei knew still referred to as Canton. She remained motionless upon the ground. Extreme caution was called for. She had certainly learned that on the docks in Canton when she'd narrowly escaped with her life.

After allowing what she considered sufficient time to pass, she left cover of the knoll which hopefully had concealed her from view of the road. She wheeled her bicycle down onto the road and started peddling in the direction of her parents' house, a half hour away. There was little traffic, most of it bicyclists who paid her no attention.

After that night of horror on the dock, she'd decided not to return to the commune. Nothing happened to her friends there, but she was not ready to return. She remained committed to the political beliefs she had come to embrace. They mirrored her hope for living in a China that continued to grow more open. She was hardly alone in her generation's questioning of a culture in which the female's main purpose was to serve the male. Everyone dressed the same. Looked the same. Talked and acted the same. Yes, it was past time for a change. Not a violent one. No! No more violence!

The slaughter she'd witnessed in Canton that night was seared into her mind and soul. That night had changed forever the quiet university student who had begun the semester as a bored, restless schoolgirl. Then she'd made friends on campus, activists in the pro-democracy underground, and had even begun dating one of them only to see him die so terribly under the soldiers' withering hail of gunfire. The hammering of the weapons. The hideous dances of death as he and the CIA man, Hagan, and even the poor taxi-driver had been mercilessly cut down.

But Dr. Kwan had not been among them! She wondered now, as she'd wondered then: what happened to the kindly old man of whom she'd become so fond?

The soldiers had come running after her. She'd fled for her life, her heart hammering wildly against her rib cage. As a supposedly respectable young lady, she hardly knew the city's waterfront. And yet her natural survival instinct had pushed her on blindly, dashing this way and that through the dark maze of warehouses that lined the docks. She would run and then hide, catching her breath. Then run again for her life. Gradually the soldiers' shouts and sounds of their boot leather pounding the pavement had faded behind her and then she'd found herself in a business district.

A line of taxis was near a metro station. She'd entered the terminal via a circuitous route, emerging onto the street as if having arrived on a train. She'd hailed one of the taxis and within the hour was safely ensconced in her parents' home.

What would they say, what would they do, if they only knew what their daughter was involved in when they thought she was spending the night studying with a girlfriend for an exam? Luckily, her mother and father were so engrossed in the events and details of their own lives that they seemed not to detect the traumatized psyche that lurked beneath the sunny façade Mei forced herself to project.

The cell phone call from Mrs. Kwan had been totally unexpected. Everything was happening so fast! Yuki Kwan had not used names over the cell phone connection, instead using a sort of semi-code but for Mei, the message was received. The physicist's wife was returning! Mei did her best to recall her impressions of the woman.

Madame Kwan had been a remote presence during her stay at the commune before the CIA man, Hagan, had overseen her extraction. Polite enough. Decades younger than her husband. Ultimately an enigmatic presence that Mei had never expected to see again. They'd exchanged no more than three or four conversations between them.

And now she was returning as she'd departed via the Pearl River. Due within hours! Since the woman had reached out to Mei, there was no way Mei could refuse. She would be meeting Yuki Kwan and a "friend" who was accompanying her within hours. Mei's stomach muscles were knotted. Her throat was dry.

She had also received calls from friends calling to discuss the civil unrest spreading outward across the country from Beijing. Something was going on! As usual, the government was keeping its citizens in the dark. Word was that a coup, a military takeover of the government, was in progress!

The telephone call that concerned her the most was the one she must now make. The pro-democracy movement had an ally in the Public Security Bureau's headquarters. It was always extremely dangerous to make contact with him. But now Mei could see no choice. She must alert him to these new developments and perhaps seek his assistance.

Was she getting in over her head? She may have

been only a teenage university student, but every heartbeat was drawing her closer to danger. Considering what she was doing and those she was associating with, if she was apprehended her punishment would likely be death.

CHAPTER 22

Dr. Kwan was amazed to see how unchanged was the place of his birth and childhood. Over the years he had often meditated on and thought about the little fishing village. And here he was, standing on this ground once again. It was like a manifestation of a dream as much as stark reality.

A few modern buildings stood among the modest adobe and stone dwellings on a high shoulder of land overlooking the sea and tiny harbor. Each house had its own small field for growing vegetables, separated by a bank of earth from rice paddies. A salt haze blanketed the coast. Fishing boats and nets lined a narrow beach. An air of desolation was underscored by the constant murmur of the sea.

The house he was born in was vacant now. A single-story structure, crudely built of stone and timber, its dark windows were like blank eyes watching him.

The scars of old charred damage had faded over the years.

Since having been brought here by his brother and the general's four-man guard detail, Dr. Kwan had been permitted to wander freely about the village under the vigilant scrutiny of his guards. They'd arrived here in two separate vehicles, the general in a military limousine and Dr. Kwan in an Army half-ton driven by one of the guards while the other three kept a close eye on him from the truck bed.

There had been no conversation between the brothers since that moment when the general had revealed himself to Dr. Kwan, who had been struck speechless by the presence of his brother. Without a word, the general had closed the door between them, leaving Kwan alone with his thoughts. They had allowed him to shower. He had been fed with decent food. His body had received enough sleep to replenish his strength if not his spirit. And yet neither his brother nor Major Zhao had put in any further appearance.

Until, that is, a short while ago when he was abruptly hustled out into the sunlight and onto the half-ton truck for the brief journey to this village overlooking the South China Sea.

The general was a commanding presence, never speaking a word, remaining once removed from the action and yet a central focus of it, wearing that little self-satisfied smile.

Dr. Kwan had formed the impression that everything that was happening, including his arrest and the slaughter that night on the dock, had quite likely been directed and overseen by his brother. The opportunity to regain his strength was merely to prepare him for this.

At last the general sauntered over to where Dr. Kwan stood gazing out across the ocean.

Dr. Kwan realized that the four sentries were nowhere in sight. He supposed the general had ordered them away for this encounter, though they would be close by. The doctor spoke first.

"I was wondering when you would step forward. Why are we here, brother?"

The general's smug smile widened.

"You will learn that soon enough. You will learn very much very soon, dear brother."

Realizing no direct answer was forthcoming, Dr. Kwan chose to change the subject. He indicated their surroundings.

"So little has changed."

"Nothing has changed," said the general.

"My life changed when you were born," said Dr. Kwan.

The general chuckled unpleasantly.

"And not for the better, eh?"

"When we look at each other," said Dr. Kwan, "we each view the same thing: the path untaken. Is that not so?"

General Kwan nodded.

"Not even a blind man would mistake one of us for the other."

"You have risen admirably high in military-rank, I grant you that."

"The process required has hardly been admirable." General Kwan's expression and tone hardened. "I have ruthlessly clawed my way to the top, would be a far better way to put it."

"I stand corrected."

"And you, the thoughtful one. The one so favored by our late mother and father." The general affected an exaggerated Mandarin dialect. "Through pure struggle and determination, my esteemed brother, an aesthete, a contemplative intellectual, has risen to the pinnacle of his country's 'scientific community'."

A pregnant silence lengthened between them.

Dr. Kwan finally said, "And so I ask again, why have I been brought here?"

"I thought it ideal for our familial reunion," said the general, "and a suitable setting for this conversation. I will need the names of anyone among your associates and colleagues with whom you have shared the Dragonfire project. We can use them."

"We?" repeated Dr. Kwan. "In the time given me to contemplate, I've considered the circumstances of my lot rather thoroughly, General. You are not operating under government sanction, are you? In my former position, I was well-informed of the imminent coup said to be brewing. You're one of the coup plotters, are you not? Considering your rank, you must be one of those behind the whole thing."

"We are returning China to the glory that is her birthright. The growing civilian protest today is meant to appear spontaneous but is happening and spreading because of our orchestration. Surely you don't approve of the way things are in China today or you would not have defected."

"It's complicated," said Dr. Kwan. "A weapon such as Dragonfire belongs in the hands of an open society that can be trusted. Yes, there is much in China that needs changing but not by military takeover. People still watch one another out of fear despite the cosmetic freedoms. The choice is clear, is it not? Do we want that, or something better? Do we live in a savage world or a civilized world? In the best of worlds, individuals are free to think for themselves."

General Kwan snarled with a wave of his hand.

"Idealistic chatter. History teaches us that the masses are unable to govern themselves without chaos being the result. Look at what is happening in America! Enforcement of civic discipline is needed to restore China's glory, not a relinquishing of it. A strong central government that demands respect, not the weakening of tradition that your sort so favors in the name of progress. You would throw away all that makes us great."

Dr. Kwan sighed.

"I noticed something rather sad as I wandered about here. Do you observe how quiet our little village is? No one is about. My childhood memory is of a warm, friendly, hard-working people struggling to survive as a community, and yet today not a single person has opened their door to come out and greet me. Do you know why that is, General? It's because they're afraid. They think I'm with you and their fear of you makes them hide in their homes, afraid to come out."

"It is the way of things," said the general. "It is the responsibility of the state not only to protect but also to offer guidance and discipline. Yes, they fear me, and they scatter when I approach. You may call it fear. I call it respect."

"As a child," said the doctor, "I remember more than once witnessing you torturing animals. I would run away. I was too timid to intercede. I would run away and be sick."

"You would run to our mother." General Kwan sneered the last word. "As you would snivel to her today if you could."

"But she and our father are not here today," said Dr. Kwan, "and that is why I have shunned you all these years. I always wondered about the fire that took them while they were sleeping. You had quarreled that afternoon."

"They should have been more lenient with me."

"Our parents may have been a poor fisherman and his wife," said the doctor, "but they possessed nobility that you could never aspire to."

Without warning the general vented a thunderous roar of rage. He flung himself at Dr. Kwan forcefully enough force to pitch them both onto the ground, the general's features flushing a beet-red as he landed on top, his hands circling around the doctor's throat. Insanity blazed in the general's eyes.

"You dare to speak that way to me, I who have always been the strongest?" He tightened his grip around his brother's throat and began squeezing. "Yield to me, you insignificant worm!"

Dr. Kwan's vision started to blur. Dots formed before his eyes. He tried to cry out his protest, but the words were choked off along with air to his lungs. His brother was choking him to death!

A sudden gunshot shattered their breathy struggle. Each brother froze in his struggles, turning in the direction of the shot that had sounded loud as a bomb going off.

A slender officer stood there. He had fired into the air to get their attention. Next to him stood another soldier who held a rifle aimed at the two brothers.

The one with the pistol spoke sharply.

"Desist, both of you! Stand!"

The brothers did as they were instructed. Dr.

Kwan tried his best to regain his senses. The fingers of his right hand massaged the reddened flesh of his throat. General Kwan, rational again, regarded with displeasure the rifle aimed at him.

"What is the meaning of this?"

"I am Captain Lim, sent by Beijing. Doctor Kwan, you are officially under arrest and will return to Beijing with me. General Kwan, I must ask, sir, what you are—"

"Silence!" General Kwan's voice cracked like a whip. "I am in command here. Order your man to lower his weapon. I would see your credentials and orders."

Lim hesitated. Uncertain. Intimidated. The soldier who had arrived with him looked as if he'd rather be anywhere else, uneasy about having been ordered to aim his rifle at a general.

Lim said, "I'm sorry, General, but I have my orders. You are under investigation for complicity in the military uprising that has begun."

Doctor Kwan tried speaking but he had not yet recovered from his brother's assault. He could not form words, only gagging, raspy noise as he tried to speak with a new urgency when he saw that the general's four-man guard unit had emerged from around a nearby house. Having withdrawn under the general's orders, they were naturally drawn back by the sound of the gunshot.

Lim and his man must have approached quietly on

foot from the opposite direction. The general's team, each armed with a rifle, was advancing noiselessly, four abreast, walking at an even, steady pace, closing in from behind on the investigator.

Doctor Kwan could not manage more than his sputtering, but he did draw Lim's attention with his frantic gesturing. Lim frowned, unsure if this was a trick of some sort. He knew otherwise when he saw the open, mocking laughter from General Kwan. That's when he and his soldier wheeled around to face the grim foursome.

A cracking volley from the rifles kicked Lim backwards off his feet. Dead when he hit the ground.

The other intruder flung his rifle aside. He fell onto his knees and waved his arms wildly in the air. In a high-pitched voice, tears streaming down his face, he begged them to spare his life. The general's soldiers laughed at him and then literally blew him into bloody pieces.

Doctor Kwan averted his eyes and kept them shut. The acrid scent of gun smoke bit his nostrils. The coarse laughter of his brother joined in with that of the riflemen. When he finally opened his eyes, it was to look away from the ghastly carnage. He again gazed out upon the ocean that stretched to infinity.

An unusual shimmering shift in the waters drew his attention.

A streamlined, tear-shaped submersible was surfacing from the depths like some shiny white, unknown deep-sea creature drawing closer to shore. At first it appeared to be the fuselage of a small private jet. When it was surfaced, the craft's six large acrylic windows lining its side indicated a private submersible aqua jet. The diminutive sub drew too much water to get closer than ten yards to the pier at the foot of a path that led down to the water. She rode the tide on a disengaged, idling engine. Its top hatch opened.

Dr. Kwan fought to maintain his mental and physical equilibrium. At last he managed to regain his voice.

"What madness is this?" he demanded.

"Come," said his brother. "It is time to leave this place."

The general made his way down the path toward the pier, leaving his brother no choice but to hurry along with him. Dr. Kwan understood that he had no choice. The guard detail crowded him from behind.

The general and his co-conspirators would love to pick a physicist's mind for more technology, no doubt along the lines of Dragonfire, to give their takeover even more of an edge. There was a practical aspect to what was happening here, yes. But was that the real reason he was being kept alive? Dr. Kwan didn't think so. The Chinese government would likely prefer him dead than see him successfully defect to the West, but his brother wanted him alive for familial reasons. He was being kept alive for the gratification of a madman's ego.

There was no familial love between them but, especially from the general, there was plenty of hate. Had the general's hatred been an obsession through all these years when they had not communicated? He wanted to flaunt his power and success in Dr. Kwan's face. Wherever he was being taken by his brother now aboard this newly arrived aqua jet, Dr. Kwan knew it would concern the coup which the general obviously intended would take him to the pinnacle of power. A military revolt in progress! Those troop carriers he'd observed in Canton would likely be carrying Major Zhao's troops into the fray at this very moment.

A rowboat was moored at the pier to cover the short distance to the aqua jet.

The general was all smiles.

"Prepare yourself, brother," he said, "for I am about to show you the future. Your phenomenal intellect notwithstanding, I am about to introduce you to the unimaginable."

He gestured for Dr. Kwan to step down into the rowboat while he undid the rope.

As for himself, Dr. Kwan saw no hope. No cause for optimism. He could not imagine what was going to happen next. At least Yuki was safe. Since this long ordeal had become his reality, at those times when his spirits would sink and even meditation didn't help, the only thing that kept him going was the love he carried in his heart for her.

CHAPTER 23

The shabby sampan forged north on the Pearl River under the thrust of its ancient motor. Traveling at a sedate twelve knots so as not to draw attention, the vessel's square stern left a broad wake behind it. Freighters of many nationalities ploughed up and down the Pearl as did fleets of junks. And there were always the military patrol boats.

Cody and Yuki made the journey out of sight, ensconced in the living quarters of Chua's vessel. The accommodations were rudimentary at best but preferable to advertising their presence as they traveled upriver. Cody periodically parted the fabric near him for an occasional view of the passing scene.

There are two Chinas. The development of the coastal cities to the exclusion of the hinterland, the gap between the registered citizens and the rural population, is severe and still widening, a split between the advanced, globalized part of the new China's economy and the vast labor force of self-employed farmers. Decades of economic progress have triggered urban development of unprecedented speed and proportion. Yet while the densely populated areas comprise five percent of China's total land area and twenty percent of its total national population, within an hour's drive of the outer reaches of any of these great metropolises, rice is still being cultivated much as it had been a thousand years ago.

Some of the countryside Cody saw was developed. They did pass provincial towns, but the region was primarily agricultural; some pastures but mostly fields of vegetables. Farmers laboring in their rice paddies. Figures clad in cotton pajamas and conical hats, busy in fields of rich wet soil. Water buffalo pulled carts and plows for the farmers.

There was a tiny transistor radio aboard the sampan. Chua had it dialed to receive tinny pop music. Yuki dialed in a government news station broadcast. She translated for Cody, which is when and how he learned about the US military buildup in the South China Sea, DEFCON 3 and the breakdown in diplomatic communications between China and the United States. The Chinese government newscasts clearly labeled the situation an act of imperialist aggression by Uncle Sam.

Cody considered contacting Washington, which

would be easy enough using the encrypted sat phone Sara had supplied him with but decided against it. He was improvising without knowing the inside intel. On the other hand, he did not need to know. His mission was to bring Dr. Kwan in out of the cold. There was no way to know where this little sailing expedition was taking him, but the doctor's wife and a sleazy river rat were as good a lead as he was likely to find. Interference from Washington at this point would, experience had taught him, likely only screw things up. *And he had his own agenda. His ultimate personal goal was never completely gone from his mind...*

Yuki prepared a simple mid-day dish of rice and noodles for them, served with green tea. She passed a serving up to Chua. The boatman gushed his gratitude. The journey upriver continued.

Thus far, Cody and Yuki conversed and shared their meal while sitting cross-legged with the transistor radio between them. The heat of the day warmed the sampan's enclosed living space. After his meal, Cody yielded to the physical reminders of his body that it was time to rest; to renew the body's strength, if not its spirit. He hadn't shut his eyes in sleep since the transatlantic flight to Hong Kong.

He stretched out on the foam pad that served as Chua's bed. He had long ago mastered the ability of allowing his body to relax completely to the point of half-sleep; physically in repose, giving the biological batteries a chance to recharge, yet with one eye slit just enough so as not become completely withdrawn from his surroundings. When on a mission, he rarely went into a deep sleep.

Yuki laid down beside him. Cody said nothing. Neither did she. The pad was just wide enough to accommodate the two of them. Cody remained on his back hands clasped behind his head. Yuki rested on her side, facing away from him.

Cody catnapped. He came wide awake when she spoke softly.

She said, "I wish everyone in the world could just get along."

The sorrow in her words was audible even through the outside river traffic noise. The thought rested in the silence between them in this close space.

Cody said, "So under all those personas, Yuki is at heart a hippie chick?"

"You mock me."

"Not me. I'd go with world peace if it came along. Trouble is, it's nowhere in sight. And if I was in some, let's say some South American gun-narco country where the rich own and control everything while the rest of us will forever be peasants in straw hats with nothing to see us through but our faith in the hereafter, well, I'd likely be pissed off enough to take up arms too and fight for a socialist revolution. As it is, I'm not fighting *for* anything. I'm here to do a job and that job is to take down the a-holes and find your husband."

She rolled over to face him, resting her head in the crook of his arm, the length of her body against his.

"It may only be a job to you. But to me and to my husband, it is life itself." She touched his face with her forefinger, tracing the line of his jaw. "You are a strong and virile man," she said close enough to his ear for him to feel the intimate warmth of her breath. "I find you very attractive. I would find a way to repay you on a. . .personal level for all you have done for me. But I cannot, you understand? I am a married woman."

She sighed. "My life is not my own. I was a graduate student in Tokyo. Doctor Kwan was a visiting lecturer. It. . .just happened between us. It was a lonely time in my life. I was adrift. I can't explain it, but I have become committed to him. I risk my life now to help you find him. But, Cody, he quickly became more a father figure to me than a lover. He is unfailingly kind and generous to me. And yet. . .I long for a virile man who will treat me the way a man shows his love to a woman. And now you come along. Do you understand?" Another warm sigh in Cody's ear. "Of course, you do. . ."

She placed her fingers to his lips. Her body was warm against his. She nuzzled against him. The scent of her filled his senses.

He felt nothing for her.

"No," he said quietly, not unkindly.

For a moment, her mask of self-confidence slipped. That was okay with Cody. The very thought of touching another woman this way would make him feel like he was cheating on Carol. She didn't know about Carol and the kids. Cody intended to keep it that way. He didn't need her sympathy and it was none of her business. He held her wrist, removing those warm, tantalizing fingers from his lips, following through in a maneuver that returned her to her other side again on the foam pad. She yielded to his direction without resistance, again facing away from him while he remained flat on his back.

And then the confined heat of the day, aided by the constant, rhythmic chugging of the sampan's engine and the sheer exhaustion of everything that had happened since his jet touched down, combined to lull Cody into deep sleep. He began to dream, knowing it was a dream but somehow that did nothing to ease its reality.

A lovely day, at first. Some national holiday. The schools were closed. He was home on leave and had taken his little family to the beach for the day.

The white sand blazed almost as brightly as the sun itself except beneath a beach umbrella where Carol lounged upon a blanket with their two youngest playing nearby with sand pails and shovels. Terri, the oldest at thirteen, was swimming. She had always been a fine swimmer. Still, when the water reached her shoulders, Cody instructed her to turn back although she was no more than a dozen meters from the beach. But Terri wanted to continue swimming with her father. She did not want to turn back. She was a bright girl, respectful of her dad but very much with a mind of her own.

Cody had never been able to refuse his children anything they wanted, and he could not refuse Terri now. She was safe enough, he reasoned. And he was a good swimmer, as was Carol; there were other swimmers and sunbathers nearby. Treading water, surveying the scene, he felt consumed by a sense of well-being. Their family was strong, and they were together. Nothing could be better. He gazed out across the ocean.

And something strange occurred with an awesome, supernatural suddenness. Gathering black storm clouds coursed across the summer sky, devouring it. The ocean was suddenly cold and rough. Not understanding, Cody experienced cold fear. He fought the waves, trying to swim toward Terri. He let out a sharp cry of terror at the sight of her disappearing beneath a cresting wave.

Terri swam as hard as she could, but the undertow slowed her, almost pulling her under. Everything had changed. Grown ominously dark. There were no swimmers. There were no sunbathers. The sand on the beach was an ominous gray.

Carol and their other two children were nowhere in sight!

Terri disappeared from his sight. And then she bobbed to the surface again, legs scissoring, his arms pumping with all her might. Cody seemed unable to make any progress toward his daughter even though the distance was short enough for him to see vividly the horrible fright and terror upon his little girl's face. He'd never felt more helpless! He cried out when he saw Terri's head disappear

*under another black wave. The undertow caught her, sucking her
down into cold black nothingness.*

Cody came awake with a start, bathed in clammy
perspiration. He blinked against the harsh light of
day. The ten-second lapse that transitioned him from
deep sleep to fully awake was a compressed kaleido-
scope of thought.

*Carol and the kids. Terri, Ty and little Gracie. His beautiful
family. So real in a dream he could touch them. But now he was
awake, and they were gone forever because of him. Because of his
negligence. He should have been there to protect his little family. He
could have prevented their death. The bastards never would have
gotten near the car to plant their bomb. Or he would have been the
one gone out to start the car before Carol drove the kids to school.
Gone forever. His fault...*

Then he was awake, those thoughts evaporating
into the slipstream of consciousness.

Chinese spoken in a rapid chatter from outside!
Gruff. Rude. A commanding voice alternating with
Chua's voice, uneasy and acquiescing. The sampan
shifted slightly as additional boots boarded.

Cody peeled back a quarter inch of fabric so he could
see outside. The sampan's motor was stilled. A military
patrol boat alongside, a .50-caliber machine gun was
mounted in its stern, manned by a young soldier aiming the mighty weapon directly at the sampan. Cody
swung his feet off the bunk, assuming a sitting position. He palmed the Beretta from its shoulder holster.

No sign of Yuki.

Then he heard her addressing the soldier on deck. He could hear their conversation, conducted in conspiratorial tones. But Cody didn't speak Chinese and so he learned nothing from eavesdropping. A few moments later, the soldier stepped back onto the patrol boat. The engine accelerated. The boat drew away.

Chua restarted the sampan's motor. They continued on.

Cody remained where he was. He holstered the Beretta. He repositioned himself in the compact space to give himself a view of the deck through the hatchway.

Yuki and Chua stood at the wheel engaged in an earnest conversation that Cody could not overhear due to the sampan's noisy old motor. Then Yuki rejoined Cody, her trim figure easily negotiating the low hatchway.

Over her shoulder, Cody noted Chua's frown as the boatman returned his attention to steering their vessel.

To start a conversation with her, Cody said, "That was close."

"Night is coming. That will make things easier."

"It always does in my line of work. So how did you get rid of the patrol boat?"

"How do you think? The oldest way there is in the

world, I would think. Chua had money. I had cash. We combined what we had to buy our way out."

"An old-fashioned bribe," said Cody. "I see why Doctor Kwan so adores you. You're a resourceful woman."

"Thank you."

She switched on the transistor radio to a traditional Chinese music station. Then, as if Cody were not sharing the confined space with her, she stretched out on the pad and closed her eyes. That was it for conversation. Yuki seemed to fall asleep.

Cody was displeased with himself for having fallen asleep. The dreams of Carol and the kids, when they came, stirred his emotions that could distract him at the wrong time. The one he'd just had was another of a recurring theme. In dream after dream the setting was always different but in each of them his family died but always in a different way. Fire. Plane crash. It was like he was being forced to constantly re-experience their loss.

This time Cody remained awake, alternately keeping an eye on Yuki and on the passing view beyond the hatchway.

Chua's sampan continued its upriver course.

They reached Canton after dark. River traffic increased ten-fold in density and noise. Cody and Yuki joined Chua on deck, casually turning away when a single patrol boat, almost lost in the nautical traffic, continued past without showing more than a routine passing interest in them.

Chua guided his humble vessel through the maze of much larger ships and boats, under Hai-Chu Bridge in downtown Canton, and passed the multi-leveled Provincial Industry Exhibition Hall before reaching a dark pier nestled amid the wharfs behind the Shi-wei-t'ang Railway Station, the spot Yuki had designated as a meeting point with Mei Cheng, the university student.

Everyone was at risk at this point.

Cody approved of the rendezvous being on the periphery of a busy section of the city, allowing their arrival to blend in with less chance of being noticed. With the current military and civil unrest spreading in the cities, the authorities would be even more vigilant than usual, primed for trouble.

During these final minutes before they parted with the boatman to go their separate ways, Cody noted a subtle shift in the dynamic between Yuki and Chua as if the boatman was more fearful of her than he was of Cody...

Chua went about tying up the sampan, Yuki watching him carefully, poised in a way that reminded Cody of a cat ready to spring. Cody glanced up and down the dark street at the end of the pier. At this hour, there was sparse bicycle traffic, nothing more.

He wanted to think he was ready for anything. He told himself that's probably what Phil Hagan thought right before his world ended.

CHAPTER 24

The sound from behind him of something sizable splashing into the water, during the brief moment his attention had been diverted, brought Cody whirling about instinctively, hitting a combat crouch. The Beretta seemed to leap into his fist. He caught a quick final glimpse of Chua's body sinking from sight into the river.

Yuki stood in a killer's crouch of her own at the lip of the deck, intently watching the boatman's shabby corpse vanish into the depths of black, oily water. Her right hand held the dagger with the wicked, curved blade. In what seemed an afterthought, she spat vehemently into the water at the exact spot where the body had gone down. She turned calmly to face Cody across the ten feet of deck that separated them.

Cody straightened his right arm, the Beretta drawing a bead on her forehead.

"Drop it," he said.

Her countenance was smooth, serene.

"Shed no tears for Chua. He was filth. If my husband is dead, it will be because of the snake I've just eliminated. Did you think I would let him live?"

"I guess not. The dagger, Yuki. Lose it."

"But we are in the city now. Inside China. My enemies are everywhere. I need protection."

"Not from me you don't. Drop the dagger, Nightwind. *Now.*"

The dagger fell to the deck, the sound lost beneath river noise.

"Then you know."

Cody nodded.

"The assassins out of Beijing just keep getting lovelier. Your original mission was to play up sweet and innocent to Doctor Kwan. You were so good at that, the old guy asked you to marry him."

"He is a very nice man, Cody. And I do respect him. You may believe me or not but that happens to be the truth."

"So what? You'd have iced him in a heartbeat if those were your orders; if the defection went too far and that was the only way to stop it. As is, you were ordered play the dutiful wife even to the point of accompanying him out of China. They didn't want him killed except as a last resort because the doc is still carrying around valuable information inside his head about Dragonfire and who knows what else. So, while you were playing the faithful wife, did you still work as an assassin?"

"When ordered to do so. I told you there were long periods of separation between us. But how did you decide I was Nightwind?"

"Come on. It doesn't play any other way. Beijing re-defined your mission once you made it to Hong Kong; after your husband went missing. You were assigned to disrupt the Hong Kong pipeline the CIA was using. That's why you killed Yu Cheng, though I'm sure you took personal pleasure in that one after the way he treated you. And that's why Chua was squirrely after we got stopped by that patrol boat."

She stared into the muzzle of the Beretta with un-blinking eyes.

"Squirrely? I do not know this word."

"Jumpy. Scared. You didn't bribe those river sol-diers. You're dressed like a coolie. Chua may have had connections, but his cover was as a poor boatman. The pair of you weren't carrying enough cash it would take to bribe a soldier. You got them out of our way by showing them your credentials, and once Chua knew you were an agent of the Chinese government, well, he was afraid you'd kill him next."

"Are you going to kill me, Cody?"

"I've thought about it. You're top-shelf talent, I'll say that for you, lady. And so young and innocent-looking too. A worthy opposite number. A worthy adversary."

"Why didn't you try to stop me after Yu Cheng?"

"Why should I? Like I was telling someone the other day, I make use of the tools at hand. That Triad boss you killed, that was understandable revenge given the way he'd mistreated you. Chua, you waited 'til my back was turned but that's okay. Who needs him? Another dead river rat. Good riddance to both of them. But you're done, Nightwind. It ends here before you get to Mei Chen."

She said, "Cody, you too show every sign of being a top-shelf assassin. If you meant to kill me, you would not be wasting time and words the way you are."

"I owe you," said Cody. "Payback for you not killing me when I got sloppy a while ago and gave you the chance."

"You mean when you fell asleep? Your sleep was troubled. I would even say tortured."

"Right. The perfect opportunity to use your dagger on me. But you chose to let me live." He lowered the pistol he'd been pointing at her. "So now I cut you slack."

"I'd received no orders to terminate you. I was vain enough to believe that you'd accepted the role I was playing."

Cody could not hold back a small chuckle.

"As the dowdy wife? That worked from a distance with photo ops and the rare social occasion but, kiddo, I saw you up close and personal at Yu Cheng's, remember? Your taste in undies doesn't match the dowdy image and you were way too smooth standing up to a boatload of soldiers. The hippie chick persona, mourning the sad state of world affairs, that was a nice touch. But up close there were just too many inconsistencies."

"What will you do with me?"

"Something that could get me in a whole mess of heat, so keep quiet about it, okay? Here it is. You let me keep my life. I'm letting you keep yours."

A Nissan drew to the curb at the far end of the pier. The driver extinguished the headlights. Two people stepped from the vehicle and began walking toward the sampan.

Yuki seemed not to notice.

She said, "You would let me walk away? But we are sworn enemies."

"Lady, don't talk me out of it," said Cody. "It's a debt I want to settle. After this, we're back to basics. Let's try to avoid each other from here on out because if we ever cross paths again, you're going down."

"You are being generous to me and I accept. But Mei and her friend. . .what will you tell them?"

"I'll think up something. Give that dagger a kick over the edge while you're at it." Cody holstered the Beretta. "Okay, here they come. For the next couple of minutes, you and I are still allies. Between here and the car, that is. I'll explain there's been a change in the plans. That's your cue to start walking. Just walk away and don't look back. Can you do that?"

Her foot nudged the dagger over the side. It sank into the black water without a trace.

"Thank you, Cody. I will always wish we had met under different circumstances."

"If we do ever see each other again," said Cody, "it'll likely be in hell. Meanwhile, stay out of my way. Now let's do this."

He turned to greet the couple.

The woman wasn't much older than twenty, if that. This would be Mei. The man wasn't but a few years older than Mei; conservatively attired in pressed slacks and shirt. A slim, intelligent looking young guy.

The girl flashed a pleasant, expectant smile when she saw Yuki who stood across the deck, slightly behind Cody. Mei started to speak a greeting when suddenly she saw something that made her expression flare into startled shock.

She cried out, "No-*don't!*"

Everything happened at once.

The young man with her had shared her pleasant demeanor upon first stepping aboard, but his expression tightened similarly and his hand dived under his jacket in a blur that could only mean he was reaching for a concealed weapon.

Instinct again spun Cody around, the Beretta again filling his fist.

The alarm in Mei's cry jolted him into a quick side-step, vacating the space he'd occupied seconds earlier. The bark of a gunshot rang out from behind him. He came around to find Yuki poised with a pistol she must have taken from Chua before she killed him. With the intently focused expression of a marksman determined to make a kill, she was tracking the piece on Cody for another shot even as Cody started tracking his Beretta on her.

Mei's male companion had the advantage of not having to draw *and* turn. He simply speed-drew and fired. His bullet drilled Yuki through the center of her smooth forehead.

She froze for a split second with a wide-eyed, open-mouth expression as if she had never been so surprised in her whole life. The neat hole in her forehead leaked a thin stream of crimson like a weeping third eye. Dead on her feet, Yuki took one, two, three faltering steps backward, her momentum sending her over the side still gripping the pistol.

Another splash and she was gone.

Mei and the man advanced to stand next to Cody with Mei in the middle. They stared down at where the dark water still rippled.

"That was...terrible," Mei said in a small, confused voice. "What happened? I thought—"

"Save it for another time," said Cody. "Short version: Missus Kwan was a Beijing assassin who thought she was smart. Hell, maybe she was. When she saw it going bad, she went for broke. I was stupid to turn my back on her. It's been a long day. My name is Jack Cody. I'm here to locate Doctor Kwan. Identify yourselves."

"I am Mei Chan. Madame Kwan contacted me. She asked me to meet her here."

Cody still gripped his Beretta. The guy standing at Mei's side hadn't holstered his gun, either.

Cody said, "And your friend?"

The guy answered for himself, making eye contact with Cody in the faint illumination of the river night lights.

"I am Lieutenant Toi."

Cody's fist tightened around the Beretta's grip.

"Lieutenant?"

Mei said in a rushed voice, "He is aligned with our movement, Mister Cody. The Lieutenant is stationed at the local Public Security Bureau headquarters. He has served our cause admirably over the years."

"And tonight," Toi added, "I serve our shared interest. I hope you will trust me, Mister Cody."

Neither man had holstered his weapon.

"Thinking about it," said Cody, "the late Missurs Kwan never got around to mentioning you."

Mei said, "That is because she did not know about

the Lieutenant. Please, sir, you must trust us. We wish only to help."

"And may I add, sir," said Toi, "that, having just saved your life, I do feel somewhat entitled to some degree of trust."

Cody made up his mind. These two combined into a potent asset. If he was making the wrong choice, he was dead. Simple as that. This world and his suffering would be over. Though he had always thought he would go out in action, in a blaze of glory, not double-crossed by a schoolgirl.

With the Beretta in his right hand, held down at his side, he extended his left hand, palm up.

He said to Toi, "I'll take your gun."

There followed a lengthy pause.

"Is that necessary?"

"It is if you want me to trust you. See, you've got to trust me too. Not as easy as it sounds, is it? Here's the deal. You get your piece back when we part ways, or if I decide you need it before then."

"But you can trust him, sir," said Mei, "you really can! The Lieutenant has risked his life to supply information. He—"

Toi said, "No, Mei. I understand. It's all right." He placed his pistol, a Chinese-made 9mm semi-automatic, in Cody's hand. "This man has no reason to trust me. He, on the other hand, has traveled halfway around the world to risk his life. It seems to me a fair proposition." To Cody he said, "I trust, sir, that you will return my weapon should we encounter personal danger tonight. And I regret to say that could happen if our luck runs out. Much is happening this night across China."

Cody thumbed on the pistol's safety. He secured the gun under his belt, concealed by his thin jacket.

"Yeah, the coup. Heard about it. That's a good reason for us to get moving. This is a noisy part of town but that doesn't mean someone hasn't called in about those gunshots. Nice to meet you both and thanks, Toi, for saving my life. Now let's *git*!"

CHAPTER 25

At Cody's direction, Toi drove. Mei sat in front beside him. This allowed Cody to keep an eye on both of them as they traveled through city streets that even at this hour were becoming busier by the minute with public transportation, bicycle and pedestrian traffic. A metropolis stirring, waking to a new day.

After clearing the idea with Cody, Toi drove to The Guangzhou People's Park, an oasis of forested greenery located in the center the city. According to Mei, it was known locally as Central Park, built in 1921 on a site that had been the location of successive regional governments for a thousand years. At this hour, the park was a slumbering island of refurbished colonial buildings, world class galleries and exhibition spaces, gardens, fountains and walking paths.

Toi parked the Nissan in a secluded spot not far from a statue that depicted a female guerrilla fighter breastfeeding her baby, a work Mei identified for Cody as The Age of Warfare.

And that was it for the polite conversation that Cody had preferred during the short drive from the river to the park. It kept his attention uncluttered and focused. He could detect no one following them. There was no noticeable increase in military presence along the way. And yet his fingertips never drifted more than inches from the Beretta.

"Tell me what you know," said Cody.

It was quite a story. The young lieutenant recounted, in precise and perfect English, the left-turn his young life had taken after Major Zhao, the commanding officer of the detachment, had brought in the much sought-after Dr. Kwan. Toi had known something was up even before this when he'd overheard snippets of conversation of men among the ranks of Zhao's chosen troops about a post-midnight massacre on the docks of Canton, executing an American CIA agent who had been orchestrating the extraction of Kwan and his wife.

Mei listened to his recitation with rapt attention, apparently hearing much of it for the first time, interrupting only to corroborate that a massacre on the docks had occurred. She briefly explained to Cody her role in that incident, how she came to witness it and fleeing for her life.

Toi continued with his story. Things happened

quickly once General Kwan arrived in Canton, to
hear Toi tell it. Cody believed what he was hearing.
With Dr. Kwan's extended detention, with the general being complicit in everything Zhao was up to
including loading his troops into trucks and heading
out, essentially evacuating the base except for a skel-
eton crew commanded by the Lieutenant, it gradually became apparent to Toi that General Kwan and
Major Zhao were highly placed co-conspirators in
the military overthrow presently in progress. Those
truckloads of Zhao's soldiers would be traveling the
long trek to Beijing as part of that coup.

Toi's account concluded with Captain Lim, a military investigator, arriving from Beijing after Zhao's
convoy had already departed and with Lim quickly
speeding off to the fishing village where the Kwan
brothers hailed from.

"And you've had no contact with Lim since he
left?" Cody asked.

"None. The helicopter that brought him in is still
at the base. The pilot has been ordered by Beijing to
await further orders."

Cody had been mentally dual tracking while
listening to the lieutenant, paying attention to and
processing every word while formulating a possible
strategy.

He said, "We can write off the investigator. He
won't be back except in a body bag. What's the status

of this base now that you're in command?"

"I've dutifully reported to Beijing," Toi said, "but they are too busy with the crisis at hand at the moment to send us replacements. I'm told the situation in Beijing is fluid."

"The helicopter pilot," said Cody. "Whose side is he on?"

"I have spoken with him. I am quite sure he is a government loyalist."

"Good to hear. Okay, Lieutenant, help me out on something. If I wanted face time with the ranking military man in China, who would that man be?"

"Our ranking military officer is General Bao, the Army Chief of Staff. But face time, I do not know this term."

Mei offered, "It means to take a meeting."

Toi frowned. He appraised Cody. Respectful. Doubtful.

"A personal meeting between you and General Bao? Sir, such a thing would be impossible. For one thing, General Bao is in Beijing."

"And we've got a helicopter pilot who will follow the general's orders, we hope. The trick is getting the general to want to see me."

Mei studied Cody with open curiosity.

"And how will you do that?"

"Doctor Kwan is defecting because of a super weapon he's developed called Dragonfire. If General Kwan is in possession of his brother, that means he's also in possession of Dragonfire. Rebels with their hands on something like that? No one wants that, not the US or China, and that gives us common ground. And that gives me something to deal with."

Toi's brow furrowed.

"I'm afraid I don't understand."

"That's okay," said Cody. "I'm making this up as we go along. Have you reported to Beijing that Lim went to that fishing village and never returned?"

"No, I have not. My concern is that our communications may have been hacked."

"Doesn't matter," said Cody. "I need you to make contact with General Bao to set up a meeting between us."

Toi's furrows deepened.

"Sir, what you suggest is out of the question. There is a chain of command! We are talking about a lowly, provincial lieutenant speaking with the Army Chief of Staff!"

Cody said, "You've got something that will get his attention. You've got me. You have an American agent in custody, and he wants to talk a deal. That's true enough. Do not reveal to them exactly where Captain Lim went after he left here. Forget all about that fishing village. Don't mention it. That's my ace in the hole. I'll offer where the Kwan brothers went in trade."

Mei was frowning.

"I do not follow this. Trade for what?"

"Answers," said Cody, "or maybe the right questions. Use your cell phone, Lieutenant. There's no time like the present. Give Beijing a call. Make it happen."

As Toi began making his call, Cody exited the car. He brought out the encrypted satellite phone that provided a secure direct link to Washington. He thumbed the single number programmed into the phone. On the other side of the planet, Sara Durell answered on the first ring.

"Well hello there. Nice of you to check in."

"I've been busy," said Cody. "I need an update."

"*You* need an update? That's rich. Last I heard, you were suiting up to take on a Triad boss in Hong Kong. What happened?"

"Old news. About that update."

Sara's sigh was crystal clear from the other side of the world.

"Update about what?"

"The situation in Beijing. I'm going in."

"You're *what?* You're in China, right?"

"Right. Beijing is in China."

"I know where Beijing is," said Sara. "I want to know where you are and what you're up to."

"Circumstance has not favored this mission so I'm upping the ante."

"And what does that mean exactly?"

"Later," said Cody. "It's either falling apart or coming together very fast. Beijing. Bring me up to speed."

"Chaos," said Sara, "and it's getting worse. Seems the conspirators have orchestrated a 'spontaneous' popular uprising. There's been a three-year famine going on over there in one of the outlying provinces that's claimed more than a million lives. They're exploiting that to stir up dissatisfaction. Tens of thousands are expected to march on Tiananmen Square like they did in 1989. The plan is for the military to use the rioting as cover to mobilize. But then the rebel generals will order their artillery and troops to turn and take over the government."

"There's a general named Kwan," said Cody. "The doctor's brother. He's one of the ringleaders. A major named Zhao is in his pocket and I imagine he's aligned himself with co-conspirators in every branch of the Chinese military."

"We're on it but with nothing substantial so far," said Sara. "What about Hagan?"

"An eye-witness saw him gunned down the night Major Zhao showed up to take charge of Doctor Kwan."

"That's not good. The situation is escalating militarily. I'm tempted to call you in."

"Fat chance," said Cody. "It'll be nice to get our hands on Doctor Kwan, but right now the top priority is defusing this coup before anything crazy happens with Dragonfire. That puts us on the same team as the boys in Beijing. I'm going there to deal. I've already got a ride, but I need you to diplomatically grease the wheels any way you can before I get there."

"Jack, that is ridiculous. They'll eat you alive."

"They might think about it. But I've got something they'll want. I've already baited the hook."

"You're going to end up like Hagan." Another crystal-clear sigh. "All right, all right. I'll do what I can if you're really going in. But what the hell are you thinking? Why won't the Chinese execute you on the spot or use you to make political hay out of a CIA operative caught in their country during a military coup. Relations between us and China would be set back a hundred years."

"I'm handing them a key piece to their puzzle," said Cody. "An army investigator from Beijing disappeared because he followed the Kwan brothers to the fishing village where they were raised. In Beijing I'm tracking down a guy named Bao."

"General Bao? Jesus, guy, he's their Army chief of staff! He's the premier's brother-in-law! You're talking the absolute top echelon of power."

"Yeah, he's the one. He's going to want to get Dragonfire away from the rebels first and foremost. He knows where the Kwan brothers are from, but he doesn't know that's where this whole thing leads. The deal is: I give them the hot lead on the fishing village and Bao initiates a database search of underwater

military requisitions and such that have been channeled through Major Zhao to that village. There will
be plenty of data if they know what to look for. This
coup is likely the culmination of years of planning
and redirection of resources."

"And what about. Doctor Kwan?"

"Sara, I can only do so much. Right now, I'm trying
to save the world."

"Jack, I've got to say Carol told me how highhand-
ed you could sometimes be, but this is the first time
I've seen it in action."

"Gotta go, Sara."

"No, Jack. Wait-"

He broke the connection.

This was the time for action, not emotion. He was
holding his emotions in check. He didn't need Sara's.
Not now. Emotion could get a man killed.

In the Nissan, Toi was just flicking off his cell
phone as Cody resumed his position in the backseat.

He said, "Well?"

Lieutenant Toi cleared his throat and attempted to
speak but only managed a slight cough that prompted
him to clear his throat a second time.

Mei had naturally overheard Toi's end of the
telephone conversation. Her youthful features were
animated with a muted fervor.

"It was quite remarkable," she told Cody. Then she
encouraged Toi. "Go on, Lieutenant. You must tell

Mister Cody what just happened."

Cody growled, "Yeah, if you don't mind." Impatience tightened his gut. "My side informs me we don't have a whole lot of time before Beijing blows wide open."

Toi found his voice, shaky at first but regaining strength with each word.

"It was quite remarkable, as Mei says. I had thought there was no chance in the world of a lowly lieutenant gaining access to General Bao. But it was as if the military crisis tonight somehow cleared me through as soon as they learned why I was calling, rather than communications becoming more difficult as I had thought they would be. When I told them where I was calling from and conveyed your message, each step along the way was only a matter of minutes before they passed me on to the next. There is much trouble there. I could hear it in General Bao's voice when he finally took my call. I say finally but really it was only a matter of minutes. Yes, most remarkable."

"Pick it up, Lieutenant. What did Bao say?"

"He has issued clearance for your flight to Beijing."

"Then what are we waiting for?"

Toi regained his efficient manner. The drive to the base passed with Mei making pleasant enough conversation speaking with noticeable pride of how the Cantonese had always been the true patriots of China who fought and died to make their country great. She spoke of seeing her boyfriend gunned down by Major

Zhao's troops when Dr. Kwan was taken into custody. She spoke with the commitment of youthful idealism underscored by the aching sadness of grief and anger.

"The Chinese people are anything but inscrutable, especially the Cantonese. We are a passionate, highly excitable people who spend most of our lives laughing and crying and *fighting!*"

Security at the Internal Security Bureau base remained lax, which suited Cody just fine. The Nissan sailed past the guard house receiving nothing more than a limp salute from the sleepy sentry when he recognized the lieutenant.

Toi drove them straight to the landing pad. The pilot sat waiting behind the controls of the helo, ready for liftoff.

Quick goodbyes.

A firm handshake from Toi, and a brothers-in-arms chuckle shared between them when Cody handed back the guy's pistol. Mei managed to see Cody off with a hug before he could stop or evade her. She stood on her tiptoes to embrace his broad shoulders. It had no effect on his male hormones but, honestly, the physical contact felt good. Then he was boarding.

The chopper lifted off.

Everything was falling into place.

Yeah, right,

Either that, Cody told himself, or he was finally setting off on his last mile...

CHAPTER 26

Far beneath the South China Sea, Dr. Kwan's anxieties, fears and concerns had been swept away by a profound sense of awe and wonder.

An underwater world!

A secret, undersea military base!

He'd again lost track of time since boarding the aqua jet that had arrived for them at the fishing village. The diminutive craft was comfortably appointed much like a private airborne jet, well-lighted and upholstered with everything from a portable bar to a video setup. The cabin had easily accommodated the Kwan brothers, the four-man bodyguard team with their rifles and the aqua jet's two-man crew.

They pierced through the water on a downward track, penetrating deeper and deeper into the ocean like a stone sent speeding into the water by a slingshot from above the surface. The jet's powerful humming was constant, modulated at a low key, accompanied by the mild, pervasive vibrations like an aircraft soaring through atmospheric resistance.

No conversation passed between the Kwans except once when the general intruded on his brother's thoughts as if he could see into them. Dr. Kwan had been staring with fascination through a circular window.

The general said, "Not an ideal way to observe marine life, moving this rapidly? You may be interested to know that we are presently traveling at a speed of 200 knots. Extraordinary, wouldn't you say, dear brother?"

Dr. Kwan did not respond in part because indeed he was overwhelmed by the assault on his senses and intellect from the moment he'd boarded the snow-white aqua jet sub.

When the aqua jet commenced slowing, he'd gotten his first look, during their final approach, of an elaborate undersea base that had been constructed beneath an overhanging natural formation on the ocean floor. His brother had promised that he was taking him to an "unimaginable future". Dr. Kwan had to admit that the general had not lied to him about *that!*

It was like something out of science fiction he'd read in his youth. He remembered first encountering Jules Verne's classic as a child. What he was experiencing at present is what his ten-year-old mind had imagined when he'd read *20,000 Leagues under the Sea!*

Then the aqua jet submarine was docking in an oversized decompression chamber. A gleaming geodesic-designed dome, lit by countless floodlights, towered above them like a giant silver mushroom on its airlock stalk.

A side door of the craft lifted while the pilot began the shutdown procedure. The general emerged first, every movement exuding the swaggering arrogance of power. Dr. Kwan did not wait to be prodded. He trailed his brother. The four soldiers filed along behind him. They came to a silvery door. It slid sideways electronically with a pneumatic hiss. The general led them along a passage and the first door hissed shut. Everything was spotless. Quiet—as in, *soundless*—except for the ever-present hum of powerful, unseen generators.

General Kwan brought them to the control room, the nerve center of the dome; a spacious, shiny metallic place of curving silver walls with the temperature kept crisp and cool. The hum of generators was louder in here. There was a glassed-in row of nuclear reactors.

The four armed soldiers withdrew, the general obviously feeling no need of a bodyguard here in the heart of his domain. And why should he? The doctor, a bookish intellectual of slight physical stature versus the general, a muscled, irrational brute? Dr. Kwan was no physical threat to his brother. Moreover, the control room was populated by a small cadre of personnel in white laboratory coats who labored over an expansive console of screen monitors, dials and switches. Beyond a curved window the sea outside showed silent and dimly green.

A structure beyond the window, well clear of the dome, caught Dr. Kwan's attention: a long structure the length of a football field with a semi-circular roof; it looked like a giant elongated Quonset hut. Great doors closed off from view whatever was inside. Miniature submarines darted back and forth between the dome and the hangar, flitting about like tiny flying saucers. Something was going on within that hangar...

Dr. Kwan understood that his brother had gone through the extreme effort of bringing him here for only one reason: to gloat. His prideful remark aboard the aqua jet was only a prelude to the rant General Kwan was now delivering, strutting about the control room, luxuriating in his boasting.

"The upper reaches of this dome," he was saying, "are administrative offices and living quarters for two hundred people who have been meticulously screened and personally selected by me. Impressive, is it not? The metal of the dome, indeed of nearly every structural piece of it, is constructed of tungsten. Is tungsten within your sphere of knowledge, Doctor? I suspect not. A square centimeter of that material can support a load of 280 tons, whereas the strongest steel can only withstand a pressure of thirty tons. After a lifetime with your nose in books, I'll bet you didn't know *that*, did you?"

"I would be lying" said Dr. Kwan, "if I did not acknowledge that, at this depth, this is a most impressive achievement."

"It is exactly that," the general agreed. "A natural formation of the seabed above us is ideal for our purpose. We have escaped detection by the most sophisticated sonar and depth recording equipment of both the Chinese and the US because the overhang returns the echoes as if it is the seabed. A base above ground would have been easily spotted and targeted by US satellites."

Dr. Kwan spoke a thought that had occurred to him since he first beheld this undersea wonder.

"I cannot quite imagine the enormous effort that must have gone into its construction."

"My associate, Admiral Yang, organized base construction," said the general. "We recruited only top Chinese scientists, oceanographers, who believed they were working on a highly compartmentalized but officially sanctioned top-secret project. They designed and built this."

"But to what end?" Dr. Kwan answered his own question. "The coup, of course."

"But of course," smirked the general. "It is happening tonight," he jerked a thumb, "up there, while we remain a secret. . .for now. Major Zhao's offensive is in progress. Admiral Yang remains so highly placed he is trusted by the Defense Minister and General Bao, the Army Chief of Staff, and moves freely among them."

Dr. Kwan's blood chilled not at the scope of his brother's perfidy or this manifestation, but with the knowledge that no matter what happened, his fate was sealed. The general was telling him everything. If the plot failed, the general would have him killed to cover his tracks unless they both went down together before a firing squad. This would not end well. His brother had the power and the weapons—one of which, Dragonfire, he had created!—and on the doctor's side for survival there was. . .what? Faith in Lao-Tzu and his Taoist philosophy? Meditation? How could that possibly be enough to rise above what had befallen him? Would he ever see Yuki again? He must never give up hope.

He heard himself say, "But, my brother, if your coup is taking place 'up there', why are we down here?"

The general snapped an order at one of the technicians at the console. He turned with a sly smile to the doctor and nodded toward the viewing window.

"Observe."

Movement at the Quonset hut-like underwater

structure drew Dr. Kwan's attention. Its great doors were splitting in two, each section sliding aside. Dr. Kwan stepped closer to the window for a better look. He peered into the brilliantly lit, elongated cavern of the structure. His eyes widened in shock at what he saw.

A pair of giant *Jin* class nuclear submarines were visible, side by side, their curved bows reminding Dr. Kwan of bullets in the chamber of a gun, waiting to be fired. He gasped loudly.

General Kwan registered a small smile.

"Diverted here by Admiral Yang covertly, armed not only with missiles but," and here the general's smile widened, "we have also outfitted them with Dragonfire, you should be proud to know. In fact, your most remarkable invention has already undergone two successful applications administered by Admiral Yang."

Dr. Kwan's chills became a queasy cramp in the pit of his stomach.

"Successful application? What. . .who. . .no! Dragonfire is not yet perfected! It is meant only as a deterrent. . .I don't understand—"

"Of course, you don't," said the general. His demeanor hardened. "While here you will perfect your contribution to warfare. You see, my brother, the coup that will bring us to power tonight is only the beginning!"

CHAPTER 27

Tiananmen Square was in flames.

When the chopper flight from Canton set down at one of the military airfields on the outskirts of Beijing, the advance phone work done by Lieutenant Toi and Sara Durell resulted in a government car waiting for Cody when his boots hit the ground.

The driver, an alert young woman officer in military uniform, briefed him on the drive into the city. The trip took longer than it should have because the streets were becoming clogged with civil unrest, more and more people making their way to the Square.

The main avenues and secondary streets were also alive with a military presence. A restless energy permeated the atmosphere. Barricades were up. Morning sunshine slanted through smoke from fires begun by the protesters.

Cody's driver at times had to back up and re-route,

improvising coolly and efficiently dodging the military and the protesters while she briefed Cody.

Anarchy ruled. More than five thousand people had already been summoned to Tiananmen Square, social media effectively instigating a 'spontaneous' uprising. Government troops were moving in. Beyond that, the driver concluded, she only knew that her orders were to personally deliver Cody to General Bao. She seemed impressed when she got to that part.

Cody took it all in without comment. He had no preplanned strategy beyond the deal he was about to offer Bao. Time being of the essence, his only option was to proceed and improvise. He was on his own. The US could hardly send him in any sort of backup.

A quarter mile from the Square, their vehicle had to stop at a checkpoint manned by heavily armed, grim-faced soldiers. There was no way to proceed or turn around. The driver showed them her orders. The officer in charge directed them to a roundabout route that would take them to an obscure rear entrance of the massive Great Hall of the People.

"I cannot spare men to accompany you," he told them, speaking in English after noting Cody's presence in the car. "It is extremely dangerous. The Great Hall's defenses have been breached by a Major Zhao. His rebel troops have taken up defensive positions and are driving back our forces. Thousands of protesters are making things difficult. The situation is fluid and volatile."

After that checkpoint they first drove through a neighborhood that appeared deceptively quiet. The absence of vehicular traffic and the shops, and residences having been boarded up, were the only indication that this was not a normal day.

Things began getting crowded and rowdy the closer they got to Tiananmen Square. They turned a corner and suddenly became part of a raging battle. All 109 acres of the Square throbbed with undefined lines of protesters clashing with soldiers. The fog of their combat punctuated by exchanges of gunfire between military units battling over possession of the same entrance the officer at the checkpoint had directed them to.

The driver had no choice but to slow down their vehicle to a crawl. Her implacable expression tightened for the first time. Her knuckles showed white on the steering wheel. They inched their way through a crowd of raucous protesters swirling around them.

The crackle of gunfire erupted from nearby. The mood of the agitated crowd was panicky. The Tiananmen Square massacre of 1989 was on everybody's mind. This shooting was an exchange between rebels and a pinned-down unit of government soldiers trying to retake this entrance.

A tank was positioned in front of an office building near the Great Hall. Cody recognized it as a Type 99.

Its big 125mm smoothbore gun was aimed straight at the rebel force. The skirmish was fierce, Major Zhao's men trading fire with loyalist troops who sought cover behind the pillars of the office building's façade. The pillars were pockmarked with bullet holes. The fire zone between the Great Hall and the office building was littered with a dozen or more corpses, some soldiers and a few civilians, pools of their blood spreading across the pavement.

Cody felt trapped, sitting with the driver in the confines of the car. He felt an imperative need to do something at once. They must find a way see General Bao.

The world exploded!

A high explosive detonation close to the driver's side was momentarily deafening and blinding, likely fired from a shoulder-held grenade launcher. The fiery blast lifted the car off its wheels and flipped it over twice, crushing fleeing protesters beneath its weight before coming to rest with the passenger side flush against the pavement.

Cody unbuckled his seatbelt. He righted himself. The driver was slumped across the steering wheel. A piece of shrapnel had sliced away the top of her head, revealing the grisly gray mush of her brains. A single eyeball remained, lifelessly observing him.

He hoisted himself from the vehicle and dropped to the pavement amid people scrambling to get away from the gunfire and carnage. He crouched low like everyone else because of the gunfire. Bullets could be heard buzzing by close overhead. He ran toward the gunfire and carnage, wishing he had more firepower than just the Beretta.

Angling in the direction of the government troops, who were directing sporadic fire at the rebel position from behind their cover of pillars and tank, he wondered why the hell the tank hadn't gone to work. The machine gunner's nest topside had been vacated. The driver sat in his armored seat in the center of the tank's hull, motionless. Cody reached the tank with enemy bullets humming all around him.

The driver's bloody brains and skull fragments glistened, plastered like a fresh mural behind where he sat. A sniper or a lucky shot had stopped his clock. His gunner had panicked and split.

Without breaking his stride, Cody made a running jump onto the steel tread of the stationary tank. From his peripheral vision he noted the Chinese infantrymen—few of them out of their teens—stationary with a fear they had a right to. Cannon-fodder, expected to give up their lives for the government they served. They watched Cody with curious, nervous eyes.

Bullets zipping everywhere about him, Cody placed an arm under each of the dead driver's arms and yanked the poor guy out of the driver's seat, tossing his corpse unceremoniously to the ground. Cody threw himself into the driver's seat where it took him a minute or so to make sense of the controls, relieved at seeing they were similar enough to the American tank he'd trained in.

Rounds were spanging off the armor only inches from his head. He knew with a strange clarity that he was closer than he'd been in months to making his final exit in battle. Chance is an impersonal thing. At any second, he could be dead as the driver. The rebels trying to hold that rear entrance saw clearly Cody inserting himself into the action and what he was up to, and so they concentrated their fire on him even as they started seeking cover.

He went to work sighting the big gun. It could be fired under both computerized and manual control. The tank carried 42 rounds including 22 in the autoloader. A mental image of that brave, efficient driver—with a third of her head blown away—spiked his mind. He triggered a round.

The tank's thunderous report boomed, echoing loudly across the Square. The explosion when the round hit was even louder. The blast sent equipment, human body parts and mortar flying helter-skelter into the air.

Cody shifted the tank into gear. The armored war machine started clanking backwards. Cody mouthed a silent curse, correcting his error. He re-shifted. The tank lurched forward to clank along ominously, inexorably, leaving a black loud of exhaust.

A cheering reached his ears. The youthful soldiers had found their balls, were quitting their places of cover and advancing along with the tank, laying down a heavy carpet of fire that took down many of the scrambling rebels. Then he heard the topside machine gun open up, the gunner having returned to rake the scene ahead with auto fire.

Return fire from the rebel force tapered off to nothing.

At the demolished entrance, Cody braked the tank to a stop. He leapt from it, hurrying through the clutter of debris. The loyalist soldiers poured in behind him. As the soldiers stormed past, several patted Cody on the back and shouted their appreciation while many others simply flashed him the international thumbs-up sign signaling their thanks and respect.

Inside, the lobby of this section of the Great Hall was deserted except for the remains of slain rebels. Three separate corridors branched out from the lobby, deeper into the building.

Soldiers under direction of their squad leaders were breaking off into smaller groups, heading off down the different routes. Everyone taking care not to step in the blood slick that made the marble floor slippery as an ice-skating rink.

Only a few seconds passed before an exchange of gunfire rattled from around a corner of one of the corridors stemming from the lobby. The Army was tasked with re-taking this building from the rebels. There would be pockets of resistance.

Cody grabbed up a rifle from beside one of the rebel bodies. He glanced around as more troops arrived. Now that military discipline had been restored, it was easy to pick out the squad leaders. He accosted one but the young man didn't speak English. Cody tried pronouncing the name 'Bao' anyway but continued to get no reaction. Luckily, another squad leader overheard. He stepped forward.

"I speak some English."

"General Bao," said Cody. "It's imperative we find him and make sure he's safe. Do you know where his office is?"

This soldier sensed Cody's genuine urgency. He did not waste time reasonably inquiring as to what an American fighting man was doing involved in this firefight.

"This way," the soldier shouted.

He signaled two other men to accompany them. The four of them ran toward a wide stairway leading upstairs.

CHAPTER 28

Cody was good with the soldier wanting to take point. He would know the shortest way to the chief of staff's office, and he was staying to the stairs. Good. Cody never felt more trapped than when in the confines of an elevator. He'd always done his best to avoid them even under the best of circumstances. In a scenario like this, an elevator could too easily become a death trap.

On the second level, a hallway of executive suites stretched the length of the wing. It was quiet as a tomb. No one in sight. Then three rebels stepped from an office at the far end, not knowing of Cody and the others until they looked in their direction. The rebels shouted in surprise and took off running toward a fire exit at the far end of the hallway. The pair of loyalist soldiers each triggered a burst that cut the rebels down, splattering the corridor walls with bullet holes and blood.

On the next landing up, the corridor looked empty until a single rebel popped from an office where he'd been hiding, waiting. He triggered a burst that stitched both the soldiers near Cody, blowing their insides all over the stairs behind and below them. Cody and their officer had enough time to hurl themselves flat upon the floor of the landing, below the rebel's line of fire. While the soldiers' bodies somersaulted down the stairs in slicks of their own blood, Cody and the Chinese soldier laid down sustained fire that reeled the rebel about wildly, literally blowing him apart in a bloody red mist.

There were the fading echoes of hammering rifles. The tinkle of brass on the floor. Blue gray haze, gun smoke wafted at chest level about the landing. Shooting could be heard from not far away. The fight to retake the Great Hall continued.

Cody thought aloud to the soldier beside him. Both men remained flattened against the floor.

"The way that guy came at us," he said, "could be he was covering someone's withdrawal. Is there another way out of the offices on this floor?"

"Yes," came the response. "In fact, that door is where I was leading you. It is General Bao's office suite."

"Let's take it," said Cody.

He admired the man even more when the guy

moved in perfect tandem with him, gaining the office doorway with the precision of a well-rehearsed team, sidestepping the burbling remains of the rebel. They paused, rifles held at the ready, to either side of the doorway. Cody reached across with his left hand, worked the door handle and eased the door inward. With a nod exchanged between them, they rushed through the doorway. Once inside they broke to either side of the door and dropped to one knee, bringing their rifles up.

They were in a reception area. Desks. Computers. File cabinets. A hallway behind the reception desk stretched past private offices to a steel exit door at the far end.

A small group of men hurrying toward the exit!

Even from this distance Cody could make out the man's distinguishing feature: a large red birthmark across his face. The guy had a firm grip on the arm of an elderly officer.

Cody's partner said, "The old man is General Bao. The one with him, they've sent out his picture. It is Major Zhao!"

Zhao was leading Bao along forcibly. The old general was not resisting. He was outnumbered and so was allowing himself to be led. Three rebel riflemen accompanied them. Everyone in that group spun around, senses flaring, at the arrival of Cody and his partner who had the advantage of the element of surprise.

Cody drilled two of the rebels and his partner took out the third one with well-placed rounds.

With his men down, Zhao wasted no time in jerking General Bao around so the elderly soldier was held in front of him as a human shield. Zhao's left forearm was across the general's throat, bracing the old man to him while his right hand pressed the muzzle of his pistol to the general's right temple. Zhao's eyes, staring out from the pronounced hue of his birthmark, blazed with the cunning of a trapped rat.

The moment hung suspended like that. A tableau of tension like the last tick of a time bomb before it explodes. The silence was taut. The office must have been soundproofed. The echoes of combat from elsewhere in the Great Hall did not penetrate. The setup was obvious. Zhao intended to negotiate; to barter with General Bao's life in order to escape.

Cody and his partner rose slowly to their feet, not wanting to incite Zhao.

Before words could be spoken, one of the fallen rebels—badly wounded but still with a spark of life left in him—propped himself on one elbow and fired a pistol. The bullet struck Cody's partner through his open mouth and cored out through the back of his skull. He got a surprised look on his face. Then his knees buckled, and he was dead when he hit the floor.

Cody triggered his rifle to take out the rebel for good. He cursed when the weapon would not fire. It was jammed! He flung aside the rifle, dodging a second shot from the rebel. The Beretta seemed to leap into Cody's hand of its own volition. He killed the rebel with a headshot.

Zhao was doing his best to take advantage of this diversion. He didn't release his human shield but inched backward while holding the general in place. Zhao leaned against a metal bar across the exit door behind him. The exit door started to open.

But Cody had recovered fast enough to extend his pistol, straight-armed, at Zhao across the distance of the thirty feet that separated them. Cody's eyes met Zhao's along the length of that extended arm. The Beretta held a steady bead on a point between Zhao's eyes, behind the general's shoulder; behind the automatic Zhao pointed at the general's head.

Bao retained a detached, self-possessed cool; more of a witness to this than a participant.

Cody said, "Go-for-broke time, Major. Release him."

Zhao sneered.

"Drop your weapon, whoever you are, or the old man dies."

Cody said two words and they weren't "good night."

He fired a single round, carefully sighted, that struck the pistol in Zhao's hand, accomplishing two things at once. The bullet busted the gun's mechanism, rendering it useless before ricocheting away, and the force of the bullet's impact on the pistol punched it back into Zhao's face hard enough to knock him off his feet.

Again, everything changed suddenly.

Loyalist troops poured in, inundating the general's office suite.

General Bao received them doing his best to appear unruffled. He nodded at the news that the Great Hall had been retaken as if he had expected no less. Major Zhao was semi-conscious on the floor, trying to sit up. Bao stood over him and delivered a swift kick that rendered Zhao unconscious. Then Bao turned to Cody through the activity buzzing around them.

"You can only be the American who thinks he has something to deal with."

"That's me," Cody admitted.

The old man studied him a moment more. Keen eyes that belied his age.

"Follow me," he instructed Cody. "It is imperative that we speak alone."

A few minutes later, Cody found himself seated across a desk from China's military chief of staff. The small office, well removed from the hubbub, had a sentry posted in the hallway outside. The general had waived the offer of his translator to join this encounter.

Bao gave the impression that this conversation would be free of red tape and for their ears alone.

Cody liked the old tiger. Most folks Bao's age would be lazing in a recliner watching Fox News. Not the general. His flesh may have been growing weak, but he still had plenty of juice.

"A woman in your CIA named Sara Durell informs me that you are a man I can trust. I am about to find out if that is true." He took his time lighting an inexpensive Chinese cigarette, fouling the air with its harsh smoke. "Frankly, I find it amazing that you and I should be having this conversation. But then this is turning out to be a most extraordinary day. And you, sir, have displayed extraordinary qualities. It should go without saying that I am most obliged to you for saving my life."

"I wanted us to have this conversation," said Cody. "I, uh, went through a fair degree of difficulty to see you. I wasn't going to let Major Zhao stop it from happening."

The hint of a smile from General Bao.

"It was fortunate for my men that the operation of a Chinese tank is numbered among your skills which I'm sure are extensive. You played a key role in averting the toppling of our government, Mister Cody. I will naturally request that the coveted Order of Chairman Mao be bestowed upon you. It is one of our highest honors."

Cody said, "I had help."

"Yes, the brave soldier who gave his life bringing

you to me. He too will be honored."

"He was one hell of a fighting man. And the woman who drove me here lost her life in the fighting. I'm glad we're on the same side. They were true warriors."

"Ah, yes. The same side. Sara Durell implied that you propose further cooperation between us. That would also be extraordinary given the current circumstance of a heightened US military presence in the South China Sea. Whether this concerns our domestic troubles remains to be seen."

"Like you say, General, I'm an extraordinary guy. And so, by the way, are you."

"Flattery, Mister Cody?"

"Statement of fact. Two professional soldiers like us should be able to deal. Why not? We both want the same thing."

"And what is that, Mister Cody?"

"We don't want Dragonfire in the hands of a madman. Let me rephrase that. General Kwan is behind this coup and he's holding his brother, your missing physicist, captive; his brother, who created Dragonfire. So, a madman already has his hands on a terrible new weapon and whatever else Doctor Kwan has stored between his ears. You and I, General—that is to say, the US and China—both want something done about that and in a hurry. Or am I wrong?"

"Kwan's days are numbered," said General Bao. "I have been reliably informed that the coup d'état has failed. Major Zhao will be made to reveal everything he knows, you may rest assured of that. After what just happened, I will likely conduct his interrogation personally. There may be some traitorous elements in the high command that have yet to be exposed. But they will be. Their day of judgment will come sooner rather than later."

"I admire your confidence and I suspect you're right," said Cody, doing his best to remain diplomatic. "But until that day comes, General Kwan is on the loose and he has possession of Dragonfire. I'm here to suggest that we work together to resolve that situation in our favor."

"You know where he is?"

"Not at the moment. But I do know that if we work together, we stand a better chance of nailing him to the barnyard door."

General Bao chuckled at the choice of words.

"What do you propose?"

Cody's proposition being a simple one, he laid it out in as few words as possible, trying his damnedest not to sound like a cable TV salesman out to sell a vacuum cleaner. He had a good idea of the Kwans' approximate whereabouts, he told the general. He shared his theory that General Kwan had established a base; a headquarters from which the coup had been launched. A staging area from which a coup could be re-launched. To construct such a base, General Kwan would have had to acquire material and considerable manpower to facilitate its construction. The process would have been well-camouflaged through bureaucratic misdirection. The Army chief of staff wielded authority superseding everyone else's. He could have the leads followed and the puzzle assembled. . .if he knew where to start. And that is what Cody was offering.

The general listened without interruption. His mind was a steel trap, processing intel and strategizing. As Cody spoke, he could see that much in the older man's eyes. The general didn't ask about what would happen after they cooperated and Dr. Kwan's defection was again up for grabs. No, the general was only interested in regaining Dragonfire and shutting down the rebels.

He said, "Your proposal is acceptable, Mister Cody. Let us begin."

There came a discreet knock at the door.

When General Bao responded, the sentry stationed outside held open the door for a nondescript, middle-aged man in uniform who carried himself with the bearing of authority as he entered the office.

"Forgive me if I'm interrupting," he said. "I only hoped to corroborate the news that you were all right, General. At last the rebels have been driven back. Many dead. Many captured."

The General nodded emphatically.

"We have them on the run," he told the new arrival, adding with a nod to Cody, "Even now, this gentleman and I are attending to final preparations. Mister Cody, allow me to introduce one of our most trusted Navy commanders. I'd like you to meet Admiral Yang."

CHAPTER 29

Two days later...

"Where the hell is Jack Cody?"

The frustration in President Harwood's words was accompanied by the slapping of an open palm down upon the tabletop for emphasis, sounding like a gunshot in the brittle quiet of the Situation Room. The three people seated at the table with him understood a rhetorical question when they heard one and so offered no response.

Sara thought, *These are the moments the public never gets to see.*

It was not about indecision. The important decisions had been made. And the public would have to be told when the time came whether failure or success was the result. But right now, was the phase that frustrated the hell out of everyone because there was nothing to do but wait.

The president said, "Perhaps I was wrong in setting an the absolute deadline."

Nothing rhetorical there. An outreach for feedback.

Chief of Staff Corbett said, "You can always call off the *Dakota*."

"After everything it took to get those old rascals in the Politburo to sign off on us taking out General Kwan unilaterally?" The president took off his glasses and massaged his eyes. "We've got a nuclear attack submarine, loaded for bear, with that undersea headquarters in its sights. There's no evidence they're aware of our presence. I know Jack Cody's life could hang in the balance if he's somehow managed to find his way down there. But we have no evidence, not even the suggestion of evidence, that he has. We only know that he's 'unaccounted for', whatever the hell that means. That's all the Chinese will cop to regarding him. As for the USS *Dakota*, it's too late to turn back now. And given what General Kwan has been up to lately and the mischief he'll likely be up to until we stop him, that's for the best. We've got to take him out. But dammit, where's Cody?"

The CIA boss, Whit Jones, said, "How the hell could anyone trip that fast from Hero of Tiananmen Square to Gone Missing without the Chinese authorities being in on it?"

"Sir," Sara interjected quietly, "Cody's not just anyone."

Jones' ebony features registered displeasure.

"That surely is true. But I do believe it's wise to penetrate their smoke and mirrors, their bullshit if you will, as best we can."

The President's brow furrowed thoughtfully.

"What are you saying, Whit?"

"Sir, those damn Chinese are responsible for our man disappearing over there no matter what they say. After what he did in Tiananmen Square, they were treating Cody like a visiting hero, which he was. The Chinese authorities were on him like white on rice. I believe they detained and possibly executed Cody."

"It could have happened that way," Sara conceded, trying her best remain objective. "We lost Phil Hagan, remember? Why shouldn't Cody be another statistic? For my money, if General Kwan is holding his brother down there and Cody's mission is to bring Doctor Kwan to us, there's a damn good chance Cody's down there too."

"In which case," said the president, "I've signed his death warrant, haven't I?"

"Sir," said Corbett, "I'd suggest another possible scenario. We can't underestimate what a rough time it's been lately for Beijing. Yes, those paranoid old guys running the country remain suspicious of our motives and involvement. And yes, diplomatic relations have deteriorated. But the initial reports to us made it clear that Jack Cody played a significant role in turning around that coup d'état. What if they're playing square with us and they really are as puzzled as we are by his disappearance? What if they share our goal to restore normalcy to the relationship between our two countries? Imprisoning or executing the American who helped prevent their coup hardly seems likely in that light, wouldn't you say?"

"I'll buy that scenario," said the president. "And yes, Sara, I agree there's a good possibility Cody is down in that undersea base the *Dakota* is getting ready to blast into oblivion. Damn, sometimes I hate this job."

"If Cody is down there and he's able," said Corbett, "he's not going to give up until his last breath. We could still get him and Doctor Kwan out of this if Cody has a miracle up his sleeve."

The president said with a sigh, "Reminds me of when I was a young pup of a lawyer just starting out. The firm I started with took on death sentence cases pro bono. Grunt work for the FNG. A year of my life. We won some, we lost some. The lost cases ended exactly like this on execution night. Nothing to do but watch the clock and wait for it to be over. . .and pray for a miracle."

Whit Jones said dryly and without enthusiasm, "I reckon this is how our boy earned his nickname Suicide."

Corbett turned to Sara.

"And the lines are open if Cody tries to reach us

in the next," he consulted his wristwatch, "fifty-seven minutes?"

Sara had liberated her cell phone from her purse upon being shown in. She raised the phone now, motioning with it.

"If he has his sat phone, it's an encrypted direct line to me. Yes, sir. That line is open."

The President nodded.

"Very good. So now it's up to Cody and no one else."

"With less than an hour to spare," said Whit Jones, "God help him. And us."

Sara thought, *And that says it all.*

The conversation moved on, the men discussing lines and etiquette of communication with the Chinese government. Sara naturally tracked their words, prepared to respond and contribute, but she was unable to keep her mind from returning to where it had been stalled for the past seventy-two hours.

Cody.

Jack wasn't the only field agent on her roster of duty assignments at Langley, but right now for her, yes, it was all about Jack Cody. The widower who'd been married to her best friend. The tormented guy carrying a world of hurt around on his shoulders. On the other side of the world. . .and they'd lost contact.

She couldn't reveal to anyone how deeply this troubled her. Their friendship and association were clear in her file. But what would these men say if they knew what she *really* wanted: the authority to put together a goddamn hard-strike team to head over there and bring him home.

Hell, yeah. She'd honcho the damn team.

But no, that would hardly play. They'd see it as too much emotional involvement and they'd reassign someone else to this. And maybe they'd be right in doing that. So, she stayed cool and collected, paying attention but with her mind busy.

Cody. What a guy. Cons the Chinese military high command into giving him a lift to Beijing just in time to take a hand in a military uprising, thanks to his abilities behind the controls of a Chinese tank. Then the guy's honored and fêted by the Chinese government that pretends to forget that Cody's first mission there was to aid in the defection of one of their leading scientists. Quite a guy.

Make that, one *hell* of man.

So, then he vanishes. Drops out of sight. Seems to totally disappear off the face of the earth. But not before bringing General Bao into the mix. Bao's massive top-priority investigation revealed everything Cody's hunch hoped it would: missiles and oceanographers, equipment and personnel; all of it channeled through Major Zhao's base outside Canton, near the fishing village through which everything—people, equipment and material—had passed, the villagers terrorized into remaining silent. General Kwan's secret base beneath the sea is located, identified and targeted. And thus far the general seemed completely unaware of this, although he certainly knew that his coup d'état had failed.

Thus far, though he had not yet brought out Dr. Kwan, Cody had succeeded in helping defuse an armed overthrow of the Chinese government and, in saving General Bao's life, had managed to nudge American-Chinese relations ahead in a positive direction by at least a decade.

But right now, the only question truly troubling Sara Durell was the one so succinctly stated by the president.

Where the hell is Jack Cody?

CHAPTER 30

When Cody first regained consciousness, it felt as if an elephant was stepping on his chest; as if he'd been eaten by a bear and shat off a cliff. The disorientation did not last long, though.

As awareness and lucidity returned, the first emotion to surge through him was anger. Anger at himself. His defenses had been way down. Nothing else explained it. He was in top physical condition and had emerged unscathed from the fireworks in Tiananmen Square. But he was no Superman. The adrenaline wind-down and the sheer drain of physical activity and exertion that he'd subjected himself to had left him at low ebb in every way.

Once the dust settled, the Chinese government had fêted, thanked and congratulated him, generally treating Cody like a visiting dignitary.

General Bao turned out to be a game, feisty old

fighting man. Cody hadn't had enough opportunity to draw a full measure of the guy, but he respected Bao as a military lifer regardless of his allegiance. He did not think the general had set him up.

Admiral Yang was quite another matter, the traitorous bastard.

Yang engaged Cody in cordial conversation as the interior of the Great Hall began returning to a semblance of normalcy in the wake of the fighting. When Bao's attention was diverted elsewhere, Yang appeared to be hospitable and cooperative, offering to share with Cody information concerning General Kwan. Cody accompanied Admiral Yang to his office.

Mistake number one.

The crafty son of a bitch had even spoken of his love of the deep undersea world of the South China Sea as he and Cody made their way through the bustling hallways of the enormous building complex. It all seemed normal enough to Cody's frayed awareness, Yang being a Navy man after all. Nothing unusual about him remarking on his love of the deep sea. The bastard. Yang must have been laughing up his sleeve.

The admiral led the way through to his private office.

Good, thought Cody. *Just the two of us. Man to man. Better this way. No one knows who to trust at a time like this.*

The admiral offered Cody a drink. They clinked

glasses. Yang took a seat behind his desk. Cody sat in a wing chair facing the desk. Yang switched on his computer. Before it could warm up, a pair of grim-visage soldiers entered the office without being announced. They positioned themselves to either side of the chair in which Cody sat.

Cody's internal warning system finally sent a belated alarm to his conscious mind. The Beretta was holstered, concealed, in its shoulder rig. He pawed for it. Flung aside his drink. Leapt to his feet.

Too late.

During the heartbeat it had taken for him to size up the two new arrivals, Yang, remaining seated and poised behind his desk, had filled his hand with a long-barreled air compression pistol. The hint of a sneer curved the corners of his thin lips.

He said, "Pleasant dreams, Mister Cody."

He squeezed the trigger. The pistol made a quiet *phhitttt!* sound. The tranquilizer dart caught Cody in the upper left chest and that was all she wrote.

The soldiers were already leaning forward to catch Cody as he lost consciousness and started to fall.

Whatever drug was delivered into his system by that dart had delivered a complete blackout during which he'd obviously been hustled away utilizing whatever devious resources were at the admiral's command. And so, Cody knew Yang was one of the conspirators, and that Bao was not. If the Army chief of staff was in on the coup d'état, Cody would have been sidelined the minute he made contact with the general rather than receiving the warm treatment he'd been granted right up until the admiral's double-cross. In all likelihood, General Bao—and everyone else on the planet!—had no idea of his present location.

Cody himself had no idea where he was!

The drug had begun wearing off within minutes of his regaining consciousness. He'd looked around. He was lying atop a comfortable, made bed. He sat up. Swung his feet to the floor. He'd been outfitted in plain white cotton slacks and shirt, sneakers and white socks.

What the hell?

He could have been in an upscale motel room. Well-lighted. Twin beds. Closets and dressers. A couple of chairs drawn up around a table. Except there was no TV. No telephone. No windows. The door was locked. No inside door-handle.

A toilet flushed behind a door.

Cody had a roommate.

He glanced around for something to use as a weapon. Nothing presented itself. He assumed a martial arts stance, ready for whatever and whoever. He relaxed when he saw the man who stepped out.

Chinese.

Age: early sixties. Wearing an identical white outfit that matched Cody's. Wispy white hair comb-over. Scraggly strands of whiskers dangled from his chin. Cody recognized him from the file pictures.

He had found Dr. Kwan.

The physicist did not look like the sort who invented and designed horrific, devastating weapons of mass destruction. Dr. Kwan exuded the mild-mannered air of one who's a whiz at chess when not adding to his butterfly collection or immersing himself in a good book.

Dr. Kwan bowed without expression.

"Greetings. We find ourselves as guests in the same comfortable prison, you and I." His eyes and manner bespoke a weary, wary soul. "Please tell me that my brother has not placed a costless chocolate you here to gain my confidence and thus my knowledge. I'm afraid that will not work."

"Name's Cody," said Cody. "No, Doc, I'm being held against my will same as you. Glad to make your acquaintance."

"I have been a prisoner for some while. My brother is General Kwan."

"I know. I know all about your brother. So, let's start with what I don't know and what I need to know. First off, where the hell are we?"

The man was not taken aback by Cody's brusque manner, which was direct but in no way hostile. Dr. Kwan's demeanor bespoke a centered spiritual serenity not dependent on surroundings or circumstance.

"We are far below the surface of the South China Sea," he told Cody. "This is a secret submarine staging area known only to the plotters of a coup. You know of their coup d'état?"

"Yeah, but no one knew about this base. The coup d'état failed, by the way."

Dr. Kwan nodded.

"But as the ringleader, my brother remains in command of those not yet identified and apprehended."

Cody massaged the spot where Admiral Yang's tranquilizer dart had struck him.

"I know. It's one of those bastards who got me down here. What are they up to from here?"

Kwan's smooth features registered a frown.

"Whatever it is, it is happening today. My brother the general is quite mad, of course. Have you ever heard of Sun Tzu?"

"An ancient Chinese military strategist who's still taught in military academies. He wrote *The Art of War* in the 5th Century BC."

"I am a habitual reader, you see," said Dr. Kwan. "And Lao Tzu? You know his name?"

"Of course. The *I Ching*."

This brought something resembling a smile to Kwan's features.

"An educated man! How refreshing. Allow me to share, if I may. I normally meditate on the *I Ching* daily but except for manuals, the only book I could find to occupy myself after being brought here was a modern edition of *The Art of War*. I have been meditating on it, and my delving into it has provided me with significant insight into the character of my brother whom I can only categorize as demonic. Tell me, Mister Cody. Your mission was to find me, is that not so?"

"That's a big part of it and here's the rest: I'm here to shake this whole damn scene apart. Or die trying."

"You will certainly have your hands full with that task," said Kwan with no sense of irony. "But sir, as to my personal situation. There is my wife, Yuki." A plea came into his eyes and voice. "That is what I must know, sir. What can you tell me about Yuki? Do you know where she is?"

Before Cody could respond, the suite's main door slid sideways into its doorframe with a sibilant hiss. This prompted Dr. Kwan to motion faintly, a silent request to ignore the question. Cody assured him with a nod.

Two rebel soldiers stormed into the suite, armed with rifles they tracked to cover Cody and the physicist.

Then General Kwan and Admiral Yang strode in.

CHAPTER 31

General Kwan ruled here. His physical stature out-
shone everyone present, including Cody. He was a
looming, swaggering behemoth. A Goliath among
shepherd boys.

The physical resemblance between the Kwan
brothers was limited to a likeness in facial features,
mostly about the eyes and cheekbones. But where Dr.
Kwan embodied a presence intellectual and aesthetic,
General Kwan displayed only a sweaty, visceral savagery that appeared to create a violent shimmer in
everything about him.

The general surveyed Cody up and down with
unconcealed contempt.

"So, this is the round-eyed son of a diseased whore
to whom I owe so much misery and suffering for
what he did to my glorious plans and organization."

"Just lending a hand," said Cody nonchalantly.

"The Chinese know what's best for them. It's about the future; revering the past while not being shackled to it. Your time has come and gone, General."

Fury flared in Kwan's features. He gestured angrily with a closed fist.

"Bah! I will watch with a hard dick while you die slowly. Then I will piss on what's left of you. What do you think of that?"

"About what I'd expect from a lowlife bottom feeder."

Admiral Yang's smooth chuckle was an oily whisper.

"Are you going to kill the dog now, my General? You would deprive him of suffering through his humiliation?"

The general hesitated, glaring at Cody. Then he relaxed.

"You're right, Admiral. Why should I deprive myself of that pleasure?"

Cody saw no reason to respond. His taunting of the general had been strategic. He didn't see much of a survival ratio in going against these two ranking savages and their bodyguards at this oceanic depth. But a man didn't just stand there and take it. You don't lean into the swing. He'd tried to stir things up; to try and gain any sort of advantage he could find open to him. So far, no luck.

Then his luck got a whole lot worse. Bad as it could get. The general ordered Cody handcuffed. While one of the bodyguards attended to that, the general addressed Yang.

"It would please me to have you accompany us upon the tour I am about to conduct for Mister Cody." He glanced at it, raising an eyebrow. "But, Admiral. . .the time has come."

Yang snapped to attention, every inch the disciplined Navy man. Except for his eyes, which gleamed more than they should have. He rendered a smart salute.

"As you say, my General. Operation Dragonfire has been initiated. I leave now to oversee our destiny!"

General Kwan returned a casual, offhand salute. Yang left them.

The tour of the underwater base lasted more than thirty minutes; a thorough walk-through that genuinely impressed Cody though he kept that to himself. The multi-level facility literally hummed with concentrated, organized activity by at least a dozen white-coated techs.

The pair of General Kwan's rifle-toting soldiers accompanied them, never shifting their eyes or their weapons from Cody, despite the fact that his hands remained cuffed behind him. Their small group also included Dr. Kwan, who said nothing yet who seemed to miss nothing as he tagged along. That was Cody's reading of the physicist; a strange one, for sure. An ally to be trusted? Cody was hoping he'd have a chance to find out.

In every area they passed through—except for the sumptuous living quarters, deserted now—screens were being avidly monitored on PCs, tablets, telephones and the line of flat screens along one wall of the control room. Pertinent security camera visuals and data readouts were being simultaneously routed in, archiving multi-layers of information.

General Kwan's strutting was that of an ill-tempered thug, completely full of himself and mean as hell.

Cody took in the sights and the general's crude bluster without comment. While filing away possible future escape routes, he found himself considering an absurdity of his own life.

Here he was, a man motivated by the darkest of impulses: a death-wish to end the psychic anguish that was his reality after the tragic, unspeakable loss of his family. One problem. Through training, experience and his own exuberance for life before that tragedy struck, he'd gone about cultivating skills and enough self-defense fallbacks that had, thus far in this mission, allowed him to counter whatever was thrown at him.

Until this moment.

The taste of defeat in his mouth and in his mind came from knowing that very soon now it could be his turn to die though hardly the death he'd been "wishing" for. Would he perish down here at the bottom of the South China Sea? Unknown? Nameless?

His reality stolen from him without his exit leaving behind any visible effect on the world? He fought despair that sought purchase in his mind.

His mission, his death-wish, had led him to *this*? Was this an understanding of dark truth bestowed upon every woman and man before they die?

When they paused for the general to brag on his "submarine hangar", well visible across the watery distance beyond the great curved viewing window, Cody encountered difficulty concealing his honest interest. The general pointed out Admiral Yang's personal aqua jet as it made its way to the hangar, which was alive with lights and activity.

Seen through the open front bay doors of the hangar, a couple of Chinese *Jin* class subs were visible, their giant rounded bows already side by side. Each submarine's dozen hatches, the missile launch tubes, were clearly visible across this distance. A subconscious quiver told Cody it was likely one or both of those sinister leviathans of the deep that had originally started this whole chain of events when first observed and reported by that Navy recon plane dispatched from the *Carl Vinson*. . .

When they entered the control room, Kwan's tech people scurried off, yielding to their fearful leader the ample open space beneath the viewing window and flat screens.

The general's meek brother had yet to speak since

the tour began. He now hugged the periphery, a cool and unreadable observer. The pair of rebel soldiers remained with their weapons trained on Cody, and Cody remained standing in the center of the control room. He had once escaped from a trap and killed four men using his feet and legs as weapons because he was then handcuffed behind his back. But he'd caught an opening that time that had not yet presented itself in the here and now.

Kwan made ample use of the open area, striding back and forth like an oversized Napoleon beneath a computerized map of this part of the world. A half-dozen cities showed blinking red lights, indicating targets chosen for nuclear annihilation.

"The missiles are armed," General Kwan enthused. "Ready to be launched! Within the hour, the world will tremble and become a changed place."

Cody said, "You really think you're going to salvage your plot to overthrow the government?"

The time had come to engage this nutcase in any way possible, hands cuffed behind the back or not. Watching for that opening. Trying to make something—anything—happen to alter what at this point seemed inevitable.

The general rambled on, likely so full of himself that he never even heard Cody speak.

"Within hours," he crowed, "China will be a *proven* nuclear world power. We will exploit Japanese non-militarism. Infighting among member nations of the new Europe is to our advantage. We will demand territorial concessions. China will reclaim Korea, Vietnam and Taiwan. Nothing has changed in the scheme of things. Admiral Yang's submarines will launch their missiles at my command." He gestured at the blinking lights on the computer map. "In the ensuing chaos and probable war, we hardliners will rise again. Our military cannot function in such a crisis without us. We will take control. Nothing can avert the coming fury."

Cody's attention was drawn then by Dr. Kwan, standing off to their side, mildly clearing his throat.

"I am haunted by the deepest sorrow." The physicist spoke in little more than a whisper. "My apologies to you, Mister Cody . . . and to the human race. I wanted no more innocent civilian lives lost to war! No more cities destroyed. The world does not need such pain." He gestured with both hands to the general. "My brother, I beseech you. End this madness before it is too late! I foolishly dreamt of creating weapons so ghastly, so horrific, that the very knowledge of their existence would preclude war forever."

General Kwan's smile was an ugly thing.

"Ah, yes," he chortled. "Deterrence." He threw his head back and laughed. "That worked with bombs and missiles, but this is not the same. Armed as they are with Dragonfire, for example, Admiral Yang's submarines are capable when on or near the surface,

of generating pulsed laser beams of sufficient intensity to destroy incoming missiles. Not to mention
melting a bothersome low flying reconnaissance
plane or a search boat and its divers."

Cody struggled in his mind against the drain of
despair.

"There's no way you'll succeed," he heard himself
saying. "Your kind never does. General, listen to your
brother. All of those innocent lives sacrificed for a
mad dream of power? Consider the obscenity of that."

The general's laugh grew coarser.

"Round-eyes, I think only of watching you die
knowing that those millions perished because you
failed."

Dr. Kwan then spoke to his brother in a voice even
softer than before.

He said, "You, my poor demented brother, are
nothing but a cowardly, frightened little piece of
chickenshit."

A short but pregnant silence followed.

The general's blathering monologue had been ring-
ing for so long in Cody's ears that, for an instant, Cody
wasn't sure he'd heard right. Then he saw the general's
reaction and he knew there was nothing wrong with
his hearing. General Kwan stumbled back like he'd
been hit between the eyes with a two-by-four.

"What's that!?" White spittle spat from his gaping
mouth. His eyes widened as if under an attack of ap-

oplexy. "What is that you just said?" he demanded in sheer disbelief.

"You heard me." Kwan spoke without inflection. "You have risen in power through deception, exploitation and murder. You are hollow. You serve a false god." The physicist nodded to Cody. "This man is more than your equal. He's traveled halfway around the world to stop you. You do not think a man like this worthy?"

The general snorted.

"He is but an insignificant foreign devil. An interloper. I am General Kwan! I fear no man. I fear *nothing!*"

"Then why is he handcuffed?" asked Dr. Kwan. "You lord over him only because two bodyguards stand here with rifles to protect you. Protect?" The physicist delivered what sounded like a mild snicker of derision. "Cody is but one-third your size and weight. And you know he is a better man, don't you, brother? That is why you fear him. You would annihilate millions of innocent unsuspecting human beings. And yet you tremble inside at the thought of this individual. Did you know that I've read your copy of *The Art of War?*"

The general blinked, caught off guard by the question but losing none of his angry bluster.

"Yes, Sun Tzu, a great man," he muttered.

"Precisely." His brother nodded. "A great man who triumphed over great odds. Not a chickenshit coward like my brother who hides behind his rank and body-guards and handcuffs."

General Kwan roared like a wounded bull. "Silence! I'll kill you for that!"

He lumbered toward the physicist, his claw-like hands going for Dr. Kwan's throat. Dr. Kwan stood resolute, his back straight.

Cody said, "Hey, General. I've got a better idea. If your brother's wrong, prove it."

The general paused in mid-stride.

He said, "Huh?"

"Your brother's right about you outclassing me in size and weight. So, take off that pistol you're wearing. Your bodyguards aren't going anywhere. They'll cut me down in an instant if you order them to. What have you got to lose? Let's me and you go a round."

The general thought about it. Then he nodded. He unbuckled and removed his pistol belt, setting the holstered gun aside.

"Yes! Yes, I will show my men," he nodded to his bodyguards, "and my puny brother why I command. No one can stop me! You and I, American pig. Right here. Right now. A fight to the death between us. Release him!"

Cody thought, *If I'm about to die, at least it will be standing up and fighting!*

CHAPTER 32

Commander Dave Ousler, USN, graduate of the US Naval Academy, Class of 2013, had a rep as one of the top officers in the Navy's modern submarine force. At the moment, though, his insides were knotted like an FNG on his first run. He had General Kwan's undersea staging area in his sights. . .and he was nursing one hell of an itchy trigger finger.

The USS *Dakota*, a Los Angeles-class sub, was the second ship of the US Navy to bear that name. A fast-attack sub, the Dakota had taken up station in the South China Sea and was presently in position at the ordered depth, held there by automatic equipment. From every indication, she remained undetected.

Ousler's boat—362-feet long and 33 feet in diameter—displaced 7000 tons so quietly and effectively as to virtually disappear into the ocean's background noise. The submarine's high-tech stealth rendered it "invisible". With all its power the total noise radiated by the ship was something less than the energy given off by a 20-watt lightbulb. From upward, downward and sideways every square foot of the Dakota's hull was being subjected to a crushing force of ten tons. But inside the Dakota's circular frames and tough welded skin existed a different world: one of regulated pressure, well-lighted with air conditioning; a world of highly trained, disciplined and intelligent young men and women; a crew of thirteen officers and 120 enlisted.

In Ousler's humble opinion, its mobility, weapons, sensors and most of all its personnel made the Dakota the finest damn SSN roaming the oceans today.

In the control room, the air was clean and fresh, the room brightly lit, full of busy people and packed with gear. In the middle of control room was a raised platform, the watch station for the officer of the deck OOD. Here Ousler commanded a full view of the Dakota's various status boards as well as the weapons consoles for the combat system to his right and ship control to his left.

No one observing Ousler would ever imagine the intensity of emotion racing through his mind and body. As an effective commander, he had early on learned the importance of compartmentalization. To those around him, and to those in the Oval Office in the White House with whom he'd been in regular communication during the past hour, he was everything he was supposed to be: cool, calm, collected and ready to launch an attack that would wipe out a nest of evil.

How could they know otherwise?

Ousler didn't see how anyone could connect the dots except through firsthand knowledge, and he was a man who'd always kept his family life to himself. No one knew, which somehow only strengthened the emotional commitment within him.

He hoped he was the only one aboard with such an emotional investiture in this. Ordinarily it would be considered a handicap, worth handing the mission over to another. But having come this far, Commander Ousler considered no option other than to accept the opportunity fate was handing him, making this not only his duty but an honor.

It had been, yeah, one hell of an hour, these past sixty minutes. It was thought an American agent could be inside that undersea base. Thing was, they— "they" being POTUS & the agent's handlers (i.e., the CIA) — were not certain if their man, Jack Cody, was inside or not.

The communications shack was located forward of the control room. Crammed into that tiny space was all the radio transmission and crypto graphic gear required to send and receive messages ranging from operational combat orders to personal family grams. Sparks ran a broad spectrum of frequencies including linkage to communications satellites. Most of the radio equipment was tied to sophisticated encryption gear designed to make it impossible for anyone but an American to read the message traffic.

POTUS & Company were agonizing over the likelihood of one of their own about to die in the coming attack. On the other hand, they could not overlook the certainty that this was the perfect opportunity to take out the bad guys. Beijing had given its full approval. The back-and-forth communication had included updates from the *Dakota* on General Kwan's staging area. Activity was intensifying. The Chinese subs were slowly but surely emerging from their hangar.

Less than five minutes remained until the deadline Ousler had been given to launch the strike.

No one would ever know of his personal involvement. This was payback. Payback on a grand and yet very personal scale. No one would ever know that Commander David Ousler was related by blood to one of the Navy pilots aboard that vanished recon flight.

Captain Sharon Davis had been his niece.

His sister's daughter.

It had been determined that the military hardliners behind the coup d'état in China had been responsible for the plane going down; for the death of Sharon and her co-pilot. And here he was, the Dakota less than five minutes from obliterating them.

He had not asked for this mission. But when it was handed to him, he did not hesitate to accept. Others might call it coincidence, if they knew. Ousler called it divine intervention. With less than five minutes until the Dakota fired its torpedoes, the deed was already good done in his mind.

Commander Ousler prided himself on having never disobeyed a direct order. Never once in his entire military career. No, he did not want to see some poor chump lose his life for being in the wrong place at the wrong time.

But nothing— *nothing!*—would prevent him from delivering retribution for Sharon.

Four more minutes. . .

CHAPTER 33

It was apparent from their expressions that General Kwan's two bodyguards were uncertain and did not know quite what to think of their commander ordering them to release the prisoner and stand back while the general and Cody fought. One of the bodyguards cautiously stepped in and freed Cody from his handcuffs, then rejoined the first bodyguard. Their eyes and rifles were trained on Cody.

Dr. Kwan remained standing to the side, having not said a word since so effectively provoking his brother into this impulsive act. The slightest trace of a smile told Cody that the physicist was satisfied with what he'd done.

The control room was cleared of everyone else.

Now it was up to Cody.

Without another word, the general came barreling in at him with all the finesse and subtlety of a freight train. Cody met the assault by launching himself into a flying drop kick, the heel of one foot pounding into Kwan's chest, the other foot smashing into the general's face in a terrific piston kick that sent both men heavily into a wall.

General Kwan threw a wild right. Cody evaded the punch with a block.

Kwan snarled, "You are afraid of me, American! I will kill you!"

"You talk too much," said Cody.

Kwan vented another primal roar and moved in fast. Cody dropped to the side, delivering a reverse elbow strike that caught the general in the mouth, breaking teeth. Gasping, blood pouring from his shattered mouth, General Kwan, snarled with pain and anger, lashing out a kick with surprising speed.

The force of the kick to his chest drove Cody into the opposite wall. With a shout of triumph, Kwan again rushed him, but Cody was ready, grabbing Kwan's arms above the elbows. He rammed a knee into Kwan's abdomen.

Kwan gasped breathlessly from the blow but managed to snap his head forward so he could butt his forehead at Cody's face. The blow missed its mark, and frontal bone met frontal bone. Both men were dazed, but Cody was more stunned as the receiver of the head butt. Kwan broke free of Cody's grip. He seized Cody's throat with both hands. His thumbs dug into Cody's windpipe. His fingers pressed into the carotid arteries in Cody's neck.

Cody clasped his hands together and thrust them between Kwan's arms, his elbows striking the general's wrists. The fingers popped away from his throat allowing Cody to chop his hands in a short, downward stroke that smashed Kwan across the bridge of his nose.

Blood squirted from Kwan's nostrils. He staggered from the blow. Cody slugged him with a hard left-hook. Kwan toppled to his hands and knees, but he managed to lash out a boot. The kick caught Cody in his left hip. He gasped and nearly lost his balance. Kwan sprang from the floor and swept a back-fisted stroke at Cody's face, following up with a side kick to the chest.

Cody managed to keep his balance. Kwan circled cautiously a few steps to the left, then rushed, coming in low. Cody put a knee into his face. A good kick. Cody had broken necks that way, caved in skulls. But Kwan just grunted and renewed his attack.

The impact of this assault sent Cody flying backwards. The fall took him by surprise. He hit on his back and the air went out of him. Big hands tried to latch around his throat. He swiveled, punching his right knee around and into Kwan's ribs while at the same time twisting out from under him. He rolled away to his feet.

Kwan stood also. Kwan rushed Cody yet again. This time Cody held his ground. His left fist shot out and hit Kwan's nose, but the behemoth kept coming. Cody followed the jab with a right cross that popped a tooth from the big guy's mouth, but that didn't stop him either. The general wrapped his arms around Cody's torso. Cody had one arm free, the other having been pinned to his side. Using his free hand, he chopped down at his assailant's nose. The blow broke the nose. More blood streamed out, but his grip only tightened.

Cody felt the pressure increasing on his chest. He was starting to see spots. With an open palm, he slapped Kwan's right ear. Kwan bellowed. The grip loosened but he still did not let go. Kwan staggered back. Cody worked both arms free. He slammed both hands down over Kwan's ears. Kwan bellowed again. Cody hit him again, the same way. And again. Kwan's grip finally loosened. Cody slipped free. He swung a hard right-cross, this time to the jaw.

The blow drove Kwan back holding his head, blood trickling from an ear. Cody had shattered his eardrums. Leaping into the air, Cody hit Kwan with a flying side kick that knocked the general staggering backwards. Cody landed and whipped his leg up and back to hit Kwan with a heel kick that broke the dazed man's jaw. Kwan wobbled back.

Cody went to his knees, reached out and grabbed

Kwan behind the knees. He jerked Kwan's feet out from beneath him. The back of Kwan's skull struck the floor with a *crack!* Cody got to his feet. He backed up two steps, then ran forward, leaped high, coiled his legs and shot out his heels as he landed on the man's ruined face.

"Die, you bastard," he panted.

He rose, working to catch his breath. He stepped back for another jump. Then he saw it would not be necessary.

Kwan was dead.

Cody had time only for one deep breath, which felt like drawing in fresh energy back into his body, instantly renewing him as he pivoted, keeping low, ready to deal with the bodyguards.

A pistol shot rang out even as he came around.

He took in the action at a glance.

One of the bodyguards, the one who had so cautiously removed Cody's handcuffs, was in the process of collapsing to the floor, the side of his head blown away in a Rorschach-like splat of blood, brains and skull fragments. Dr. Kwan was in the progress of turning from this to face Cody.

The physicist held a pistol with smoke curling from its muzzle. He had grabbed the pistol set aside by General Kwan before the fight. The bodyguards had been transfixed by the sight of their CO taking a fatal beating and this had cost one of them his life.

Everything was happening in a fast blur.

Dr. Kwan tossed the pistol to Cody even as he was diving for cover because the surviving bodyguard was in the process of tracking his rifle on him. The soldier triggered a 3-round burst, ear-hammering in the confines of the control room, leaving an irregular set of bullet holes in the wall behind Dr. Kwan, missing him by inches because the physicist pressed himself against the floor.

Even as he triggered the burst, the soldier saw Cody catch the pistol tossed and so promptly forgot about Dr. Kwan, tracking his rifle at Cody. But by that time Cody had already flung himself defensively to the floor and was triggering rounds. Three bullets from the pistol—a 9mm Type 92 semi-automatic—punched into the soldier's chest and dropped him dead. Cody shoved the pistol into his pants pocket. He rushed over to grab up one of the dropped assault rifles.

Dr. Kwan lifted himself and left his place of cover. He joined Cody.

Cody said, "Let's get the hell out of here. The aqua jets!"

Dr. Kwan nodded. The docking area had been part of the general's tour. They started out of the control room without Dr. Kwan casting even a single glance at the battered remains of his brother.

Cody paused only long enough for a glance up at

the flat monitor screens lining the wall. The middle screen showed Admiral Yang's two submarines emerging from their hangar. Cody cursed vehemently. He triggered a parting burst from the assault rifle in nothing but sheer frustration, then he exited. His parting view of the control room was of the screens and equipment being shattered, blown to pieces.

Cody and the physicist hurried to where aqua jets were docked. No one tried to stop them in the hallways of the HQ. Faces of the white-smocked, unarmed technicians who had signed on for this Armageddon project, peered at their passing, drawn but frightened by the ruckus in the control room. Cody paid them no mind.

Was he too late?

Had he survived another mission only to witness the destruction of the civilized world?

✻✻✻

Aboard the Dakota, the fire control technician had processed the necessary presets into the two torpedoes Commander Ousler had ordered up for the hit, accomplished entirely at the console. The weapons were loaded with the required data, made ready in every respect with the outer doors open. Ready to be fired.

Ousler remained visibly calm as he issued the commands.

"Firing point procedures, Master 1, tubes one and two."

"Aye, sir," came the prompt response from the torpedo room.

An operator reported the relevant target data.

"Match sonar bearings and shoot, tubes one and two."

"Match sonar bearing, tubes one and two, aye, sir."

"Fire one and two."

Ousler's voice was steady.

The fire control coordinator repeated the command. The torpedoes were launched, forcefully ejected from their tubes. Their fuel engines came to life, powering their powerful pump jets.

"Tubes one and two fired," confirmed the weapons control officer.

As the torpedoes picked up speed, racing toward their targets, Commander Dave Ousler experienced a profound sense of release and justification.

He whispered to himself and no one else, "This belongs to you, Sharon. *Payback!*"

CHAPTER 34

When the massive underwater explosion erupted, the aqua jet carrying Cody and Dr. Kwan had sped far enough out of staging area to escape the epicenter of the blast but was still close enough to be engulfed by the immense repercussions rupturing the depths. Those violent repercussions spun and flung the aqua jet about like a toy discarded by a petulant child.

There had been a delay in boarding in the form of two soldiers guarding the line of aqua jet transports that serviced the main HQ with the submarine hangar. Cody had flung Kwan bodily to the floor and then covered his frail body with his own as he returned fire with the soldiers. Only his lightning reflexes and marksmanship allowed for he and Dr. Kwan to hustle past their bodies moments later, and shortly after that they were boarding the craft that was capable of reaching speeds of 200 knots per hour.

Dr. Kwan had paid attention on his aqua jet arrival and so he knew how to go about securing the hatch while Cody made a fast study of the controls. The craft bore Chinese military markings but, much like the tank in Tiananmen Square, the actual controls largely conformed to a universal arrangement. He and Kwan buckled themselves in and were on their way.

Until the mega-blast.

There was absolutely no way for Cody to maintain or regain control of the small craft under such tumultuous conditions. They were helplessly carried along flipping and twisting under the incredible power pulses expanding from the destruction of the base.

***

Admiral Yang sat at his command console as the stern of his submarine cleared the hangar. He was experiencing a nearly overwhelming level of pleasure and anticipation. He hadn't felt this exhilarated since watching the American reconnaissance plane melt under the awesome power of Dragonfire.

This was almost better than the pride he'd taken in turning the tables on the American, Jack Cody.

But nothing matched the feeling that now possessed him. It had begun. His destiny, his eternal place in the history of China, was about to be secured. This time they would not fail. How could they, with the element of surprise and a weapon like Dragonfire?

When it came, the mega-explosion ripped apart both submarines, fragmenting them. Destroying everything and everyone aboard.

Sending it all to the bottom of the sea.

✳✳✳

The mighty *USS Dakota* had shuddered through her length with the first sudden expulsion of compressed air that ejected the torpedoes into the seawater.

Those aboard were ready for what followed, expecting the rumbling fury of sound produced by the awesome mega-blast. It was more than the ship's sonar personnel could withstand. They yanked off their headset, turning down the speaker volume and watching their sonar consoles illuminate.

In the control room and sonar room, Commander Ousler and his crew witnessed the carnage in somber, professional silence as the undersea HQ, the two subs and their hangar were all decimated.

Beneath the satisfaction he felt with the success of the mission, the performance of his crew and achieving his personal goal—his niece, Captain Sharon Davis USN, had been avenged and could now rest in peace—beneath all of that was the lingering hope Davis nursed that the CIA guy, Cody, had somehow not been caught in the destruction.

***

The intensity of the underwater impulses from the explosion gradually diminished over a brief time and considerable distance, allowing Cody to regain control of the aqua jet. It took him a few minutes beyond that to recover from the disorienting wild ride.

Dr. Kwan took a little longer, although the elderly physicist did appear to regain his demeanor of centered, erudite sophistication in relatively short order.

Cody went about determining their location and course. It would now be only a matter of making radio contact for pickup from a Navy vessel or helicopter. That wouldn't take long given the increased US presence in the area.

"How are you doing, Doc?"

"I feel as if I have finally and truly achieved independence," said Dr. Kwan. "I owe it all to you, sir. Thank you."

"You did your part," Cody assured him. "That business of goading your brother into going one on one with me is what turned the trick. Using Sun Tzu and *The Art of War* against the general was a nice touch."

Kwan smiled his small smile.

"The *I Ching* advises us that everything we need is naturally provided for. In this case, that was Sun Tzu and it was my brother who provided the book. I merely found a way to make use of what was there. But now, Mister Cody, if I may. . .there is one matter still pressing upon me. My wife, Yuki. What has become of her? Where is she?"

Cody said, "Sad to say, Doc, that's a long story. . ."

EPILOGUE

It was the morning following Dr. Kwan's arrival on the *SS Carl Vinson.*

On the deck of the carrier, Cody and Sara Durell stood at the rail, watching the choppy waters of the South China Sea pass by far below them. Cody had slept straight through for eleven hours once the Navy helo touched down; the first decent rest he'd gotten since the mission began.

Sara had been airlifted in during the night to personally oversee Dr. Kwan's debriefing and transfer to the States.

"How are you, Jack?"

Should he tell her the truth? Despite being well rested or perhaps because of it, he felt nothing but an aching weariness. An unspeakable loneliness. But there was no reason to tell Sara that.

He said, "It's another day. How's the doc?"

"I had him put on a suicide watch last night just in case but so far, so good. He has requested that the debriefing proper not begin until we're returned on American soil. That's under consideration. He seems healthy enough but apparently, he loved his wife very much. He told us you related to him everything that happened to his wife. Everything."

"I only told him the truth. He deserves to know the truth. Everyone does."

"The Canton police recovered her body from the river. When I told Doctor Kwan, he told me that his heart bleeds tears of blood."

Cody said, with the merest touch of irony, "Deception thy name is woman."

Sara tentatively placed a hand lightly upon his wrist.

"Love can break a heart," she acknowledged. "But, Cody, think about it. Love can heal the heart."

He wished she hadn't said that.

"I don't think about love, Sara. I can't. Hell, a man's supposed to feel something after he's done the things I've been doing. After killing all those men. Not me. I feel nothing for the men I've killed except envy."

She studied him for a length of time before saying, "Dear, Jack, you're not a man to live the rest of your life thinking that way. You need to rethink this. Really. You've just played a major role in stabilizing world peace and advancing human rights in China, and damn if they don't have a ceremony scheduled for you in Beijing next month. That old General Bao talks about you the way a father feels pride for a son. You're going to die soon enough, Suicide Cody. Stop striving for what comes to all of us when it's our time. You've been working at getting killed. It's time for you to work at living."

"And if I don't? You think one measly life can make a difference?"

"I don't *think* it," said Sara. "I *know* it. Sure, a human lifespan is only a grain of sand in eternity. But let enough grains of sand activate over enough time and you have a Grand Canyon. Enough shoulders to the evolutionary wheel *will* change the world for the better. Yes, I *know* that in my heart where it counts. That's the life a man like you is born to live, and the purpose."

He turned from looking into her eyes and stared out across the sea. He knew she had feelings for him. Sara was a good woman who *cared*. He wondered if what he saw in her eyes wasn't that same soul-weary loneliness he felt. He didn't know what to say and so he said nothing.

When it became obvious that he wasn't going to respond, Sara's tone returned to cool and professional.

She said, "Okay, Jack, maybe this will cheer you up. I have your next mission."

A LOOK AT: CAMP DAVID HAS FALLEN
(CODY'S WAR BOOK TWO)

THE MODERN MASTER OF THE ACTION ADVENTURE M.I.A. HUNTER SERIES TAKES YOU TO CAMP DAVID!
Camp David ranks with the White House and Air Force One as the most secure military site in America. Located in the rugged hills of Maryland 60 miles northwest of Washington, Camp David is the private country retreat for the President, his staff and family and also the perfect setting for affairs classified as too sensitive for public consumption.

When the Israeli prime minister visits Camp David for a summit meeting with POTUS, the stakes are high enough for a highly trained team of terrorist assassins to perform the impossible. They penetrate Camp David's security. Chaos, fire fights, explosions, death and deception transform the rugged terrain into a wholesale killing ground.

"One of the best adventure writers of our time!" - James M. Reasoner, NYT Bestselling author.

AVAILABLE NOVEMBER 2019 FROM STEPHEN MERTZ AND WOLFPACK PUBLISHING.

ABOUT THE AUTHOR

Stephen Mertz is an American fiction author who is best known for his mainstream thrillers and novels of suspense. His work covers a wide variety of styles from paranormal dark suspense (Night Wind and Devil Creek) to historical speculative thrillers (Blood Red Sun) and hardboiled noir (Fade to Tomorrow). Mertz is also a popular lecturer on the craft of writing and has appeared as a guest speaker before writer's groups and at universities.

Steve's writing output increased dramatically when he emerged as one of the country's most in-demand writers of adventure paperback novels, averaging four books per year for ten years. His work on Don Pendleton's Mack Bolan series is regarded by fans as some of the best in that series. He also created the Mark Stone: MIA Hunter and Cody's Army series, written under the pseudonyms Jack Buchanan and Jim Case respectively.

Stephen Mertz lives in the American Southwest, and he is always at work on a new book.

Find Stephen online: www.stephenmertz.com